CHINESE MEMORIES

Olivia Xiaoyu Wang Ph.D.

ISBN: 1944129006
ISBN 13: 9781944129002
Library of Congress Control Number: 2016909555
con.fuci.us, Slingerlands, NY

To my boys:
My husband, Hao, whose talents and capabilities inspire me and whose
unwavering support sustains me;
My older son, Juneau, who will change the world for the better and whose
faithful encouragement and editing of my book made it all happen;
My younger son, Alex, whose love makes my heart soar...

To people who love and support me:
My immense gratitude goes to you.

CONTENTS

CHAPTER 1
MILK AND RATION

Memories are like a kaleidoscope. If you look closely, they sparkle. And if you change your perspective, they turn into something else completely.

I remember we started out in a summer storm, taking my new baby sister to our new residence at Number 9 Din Yin Hutong (Street). However, when our family got there, the clouds had broken, and the afternoon sun was shining through the leaves of the date trees. A rainbow reflection hung invitingly on the window of our new apartment.

My sandals clapped on the pooling rain in the brick-laid courtyard, like the sound of trumpets welcoming me to my new fairyland. Up on the northwest side, my new home was the one shining mesmerizingly in the rainbow.

Ding Yin Hutong is famous. Just a couple of gates down was Number 13 Ding Yin, where the famous Courtesan Su San used to live before she went to jail on false charges, but eventually she was rescued by her true love.

In the old days, Beijing streets were filled with both the wealthy and the poor. In simple terms, residences were categorized as courtyards and mixed yards. In the mixed yards resided the poor. Directions and boundaries were often blurred. But a courtyard was typically occupied by a single family, often the well off. The different sides of the courtyard were meant for specific people to live in. The family head and heir apparent resided in the north quadrant. It often had steps leading up to the center-north room, where either the head of the household resided or a temple for the ancestors was placed. Concubines traditionally occupied the east and west sides of the courtyard. The south side, however, was often for servants.

No. 9 Din Yin was a regular courtyard type of Beijing's traditional residence. After the Chinese revolution of 1949, all land and real estate had been confiscated by the government. The center room of the north quadrant now housed Granny Su, the previous owner of Number 9. Her son, Uncle Su; his wife; and a son named Tong occupied the northeast room. A retired couple, Mr. and Mrs. Qin, occupied the west, and an old lady in her seventies with bound feet, Granny Gu, occupied the east. On the south side, Granny and Grandpa Liang, with their two sons and one daughter, occupied the three-room suite.

Although all the neighbors seemed harmless, it took me a while to know where to place my trust. As an older sibling, I felt the need to protect my little one.

My sister must have been the most beautiful baby in the world. She had chubby baby cheeks—all pink and dimpled—short, fine baby hair; twinkling eyes; and an all-gum smile. She was always smiling when I was around—*especially* when I was around. She would even turn her head to follow me with her toothless grins. I adored her. I thought she was mine. *My baby*, I thought. I was just over two years old. However, I have remembered my sister's baby look so well that I keep seeing her image in my children nowadays. My parents told me that a neighbor had commented on how darling my baby sister was and jokingly said that he was going to take her as his. I dashed home and covered my sister with blankets and pillows so that he could not find her and take her away from me. Luckily, my parents followed me and rescued my sister from the potential suffocation of my love.

As soon as my sister could sit up, I started to let her ride on me. For years and years afterward, I enjoyed being Nan-Nan's horse. Nan-Nan is her name. I felt useful to her. That was the most important thing to me at that age.

My sister and I were almost exactly two years apart. At the time in Beijing, the best-supplied city of all China, children under the age of two had a ration of one pound of fresh milk each day. I did not know about the ration stuff. In my mind, there was always a pound of milk, and because I had a baby sister now, she should have the milk. I happily accepted that fact...until one day, I smelled it—the sweet richness filling the room with allure.

We were playing hide-and-seek on the bed. She raised herself up, giggling, peeling the pillow cover away from my hiding face. It was at that moment that my nostrils were permeated with the delicious, sweet smell of milk, and it tickled all my senses.

My eyes darted over our one room with kitchen nook apartment. Sitting temptingly on the edge of the stove was a small aluminum pot which was cooling down the just-boiled milk. It gave out the fragrance like an enchantment. The scent climbed over the sofa chairs that Mom and Dad made using old tires, recycled wood and left over fabrics from our curtains; the scent crawled across our meticulously protected burr wood-inlaid heirloom writing desk. It drew me over like magic and I found myself holding the pot and gazing into the content. It was the most beautiful shade of white with a tint of cream color. It shimmered with opulence. I held it and admired it—a film of milk breaking at the edges where it met the pot. I heard giggling behind and turned around. My baby sister thought we were still playing. She ducked her head behind the quilts.

But it was I who decided to hide, really hide, under the big writing desk, tightly holding the milk pot. I did not know where our nanny was, maybe cooking outside or getting water. I might have held the pot a long time until I thought to myself, *Just one taste, nothing more. Just one taste to see if it is still like I remember.* So I did. The tender, sumptuous liquid rolled down my tongue to my throat, and the creamy sweetness lingered in my mouth. It tasted even better than I had remembered. I thought next that I should lick away the milk film because Nanny would have done that anyway before giving it to my baby. I cherished the whole process, especially the part where I licked the stuck film on my lips. I was ready to come out and put the milk pot back, but my throat felt so dry after swallowing the film. *A small sip*, I thought, *to soothe my throat.*

In reality, however, it was a big gulp. After that, the thought of putting the milk pot back made my tummy a little angry. The next moment turned a little hazy. As if famine seized me, I devoured the milk with raging gusto. When I inspected the pot, I was shocked to see how very shallow the milk level was right now, semi translucent, revealing the bottom of the pot. I knew that I could not put it back and pretend nothing had happened anymore. Moreover, I knew that I had done something terribly wrong. With nothing else to lose, I triumphantly downed the milk and walked out from under the desk to face the music.

What happened next confused me a lot. Our gentle nanny fussed about no more milk for the baby. She grumbled at me in her forever-soft tone, letting me know what an inconsiderate child I had been. My mom, on the other hand, hugged me with teary eyes and reassured me that everything was OK and that I did not do anything wrong. She hugged me many more times that night after she made sugared rice porridge for my sister. My father seemed quite desolate that evening. He paced around as if he was preoccupied. He sometimes sighed loudly, like a deflating tire. He did not seem like the confident, warmhearted man he had always been. When I woke up at my normal 2:00 a.m. (yes, I was like that my whole childhood), my parents were still talking. When my mom saw me waking up, she picked me up and held me tight until I fell asleep again.

Ever since then, my sister and I always seemed to have milk whenever we wanted. However, my parents constantly reminded us that we should not discuss with people what we ate and where we had gotten it. As I got older, I learned the power of ration coupons: the simple tickets that, while meant to distribute scarce resources of food evenly over a great nation, had far greater hidden values of their own.

CHAPTER 2
WHERE ARE YOU, GRAY-GRAY?

E ven though the official elementary-school age was seven, my parents thought I was ready when I turned six. During that time in China, school started right after the Chinese New Year, in the deep cold of winter. Mom and Dad went and talked to the principal and the teachers. Then there I was, a first grader. I did not like it very much, because not only was it cold, but it also meant that I had to walk past a particular place at least twice a day.

Along Ding Yin Street, where an adjoining street made a T, a huge pile of garbage always accumulated. That was the official trash dump for the neighborhood. Although there were some containers lined against the street wall, trash was always overflowing: random paper, books and boxes, dirty rags and scrap cloth, rotten cabbages and smelly turnips, rancid bones and carcasses from someone's meal…Every time I had to walk by, I always pinched my nose tightly, sneaking along the opposite side of the street, almost shrinking into the wall to pass.

On one of the dark, cloudy spring days, I hastened my steps, trying to pass the trash dump to get home. However, this time a girl, and whatever she was doing caught my attention and eventually stopped me in my tracks. Her back was facing me. She wore a white short-sleeved shirt with a green military-issued skirt. Her yellowish hair slipped against her back as she ducked her head into one of the trash containers.

As I watched more closely, I saw she was actually standing on an empty wooden crate. In her hand that was reaching into the Dumpster, there appeared to be something wooden, too.

"What...what are you doing there?" She looked so neat; that was why I had to intervene.

"Oh, me?" She turned around and looked at me, her fair complexion flushed and sweaty. "Come and give me a hand. A kitten fell into the Dumpster."

"A kitten?" I ran forward and then stopped midway, resuming my nose-pinching position, but eventually I stepped toward her again.

She waved to me impatiently. I gave in and climbed onto the wooden crate, too. The Dumpster was mostly empty, and I could see a gray little fur ball hunched all the way in the back corner, the girl's wooden stick barely long enough to reach her.

"How can you get the kitten out with a stick?" I gave her a look and started to look around my trash surroundings. There were some dirty ropes lying around and some more wooden crates, broken. I jumped down and tied the ropes snuggly around a crate, all the time thinking how to wash my hands afterward. After lowering it into the Dumpster, I helped the girl gently push the shivering kitten into the crate. Then the crate was airborne, and soon enough, the tiny little kitten was in our hands.

Subconsciously I looked at my hands and then the kitten, wondering which was dirtier. But the little fuzzy fur ball was so cute that I forgot my hygiene standards. Her eyes were a sparkly jet-black color, and she had gray fur all over her except for her nose tip and a triangular white spot right under her chin.

"We shall call her Gray-Gray," the girl said. "By the way, I am Yung-Hong (Forever Red)."

"My name is Morning Feather. We should give her some food. She looks scared."

Yung-Hong smiled. "Yes, but a bath first." I hurriedly agreed.

"Come on, my house is right there." She pointed to the huge red doors with giant steps and statues of two lions guarding on each side. I stopped before proceeding. "You live here?"

"For now."

"So your family's military."

"Mmhmm…"

"I have never been here before. You guys don't like visitors. The doors are always closed during the day."

"That's because nobody ever stayed long enough to get to know anybody here. The residents here change all the time. That's why you don't see visitors or neighbors."

"How long have you been here?"

"A couple of weeks, I think."

"How long are you staying?"

"I don't know. I never know…But I hope, forever."

She gave me a brilliant smile and took my arm. We walked up the steps, opened the red doors, and then stepped down into the grand courtyard. It was rectangular with slate flooring. Groomed potted plants surrounded two big trees in the middle.

I could not immediately tell how many homes were here. The center one on the north side seemed huge, with multiple rooms on either side. The east and west sides could have a few homes each. We entered the first door on the west side. The rooms were much larger than the ones I lived in.

The center was a living room; it had a tall ceiling with carved wooden beams. The furniture was mission style. Mahogany-colored sofa chairs and a coffee table sat silently, strong, bare, and uninviting—maybe because none of them had any cushions on it. The grand room felt empty and cold, despite the reddish color of the furniture. I kept thinking something was missing but could not figure out what.

"Come with me," she said and led me into the room to the left, which functioned as a kitchen. Compared to mine, this kitchen was humongous.

Once inside the kitchen, I saw many crates stacked together. The fragrance gave away the contents of apples, and if you looked closer, some apples actually seemed to peep at you. She walked left to the big water jug, a staple in every house. She opened it and grunted, "Oh, snap." I went to look. The jug had about two inches of water left on the bottom, which would be very difficult for either of us to get out.

She grabbed the bucket. "Wait for me."

"I am coming, too." I followed her into the courtyard again and helped her get water from the faucet by the trees and carry it back to the main room.

We poured most of it into the water jug and the remainder into a big aluminum bowl.

Now I realized that Gray-Gray had been sitting on my shoulders. Yung-Hong poured some hot water into the bowl, too, and got soap. She tried to lift Gray-Gray from me, but Gray-Gray got scared, and her nails locked tightly onto my shirt.

"Can I have a towel?" I asked.

She fetched a white one with blue stripes, another military issue. I dipped it in the bowl, wrung it half dry, and gently covered Gray-Gray's little body with the warm towel. She quieted down, enjoying the damp warmth, and trustingly nestled her head into the groove of my neck. Yung-Hong watched as if mesmerized.

I put the towel-wrapped Gray-Gray gently into Yung-Hong's lap. She held her still as if in a trance. Then Gray-Gray moved to get out of the towel.

"I think the towel is getting cold." I tested the water in the bowl and poured a little more hot water in.

This time Gray-Gray obliged and allowed me to lower her into the bowl. She had the most sparkly black eyes I had ever seen. I thought cats had green, blue, or yellow eyes before. Hers were really like mine. They shone innocently against her gray fur—now I noticed some white and black hair mixed within. I wondered what she was going to look like when she grew up. She flipped over in the shallow water, exposing a little of her tummy, sticking out her tongue to lick her paws. I took it as a cue to rub her tummy with soapy water. She meowed with satisfaction.

Yung-Hong looked on with amazement. However, I knew I was trying to figure out something else, at every wave of Yung-Hong's sandy hair.

Then Gray-Gray straightened up. I guessed she was done. I dried her off with another blue-striped towel and put her on the kitchen table, which was quite small and lower than a school desk. Gray-Gray walked to the edge. With one measuring look, she bravely jumped to the floor and started wandering around.

"Let her be," we said simultaneously and smiled at each other at the synchrony.

"Here, apples. I hope you like them." Yung-Hong put a big one into my hand, half red and half green, a small leaf on the stem. It glistened in the afternoon sun.

"Thank you. It looks gorgeous." I admired it.

"There're loads more." She pointed to the crates stacked high along the southern wall.

Now I suddenly figured out what I was thinking every time I looked at Yung-Hong's hair.

I bit deeply into the flesh of the apple and let the sweet, tart juice sink into the roots of my teeth, a sensation so rare.

"Come to my house tomorrow; I have something to share with you, too. Bring Gray-Gray," I said.

A lighthearted whistle blew in the yard, only to bring a cloud over Yung-Hong's face. "Dinner is here."

"What's wrong?" I asked.

"Nothing," She went to open the door. A young soldier, still looking like a teenager, came in with a big wooden box. He opened it, unloaded four dishes onto the living room dining table, and left.

"I should go now." I picked up Gray-Gray to pet her.

"I know," Yung-Hong said gloomily. "Gray-Gray will keep me company here," she added. Then all of a sudden, she became unsure and looked at me anxiously.

"Of course." I handed Gray-Gray to her. She seemed relieved. "When do you get off school?" I asked.

"Three thirty p.m."

"I live in number nine. Come to my place at three thirty."

"You bet." She was beaming.

When I got home, Mom had just started cooking. I went to help her and told her about Yung-Hong, Gray-Gray, her house, and the apples…I asked if Mom could make an extra black sesame cake that night. I saved mine and the extra one for Yung-Hong's visit.

The next day after school, I ran all the way to my house. Yung-Hong was waiting, Gray-Gray in her arms. She waved to me as I approached and Gray-Gray jumped down to greet me.

The three of us ran into our courtyard.

A shocking scene stopped Yung-Hong in her tracks. Kneeling on a washing board, with the ridges and valleys of the board cutting into his skin, was Tong Su, Uncle Su's son. Before I could stop Yung-Hong, she ran up to him. "Are you OK? What are you doing?" she asked concerned.

"Get the hell out of here. It's none of your business," Tong cursed her in a rough, cracked tone.

I pulled Yung-Hong away and into my house.

"What the heck, Morning Feather? What's going on?"

I knew Yung-Hong was upset. I shared with her the truth. "That's Tong. He is actually a year younger than we are. His father is very harsh. He often punishes Tong for whatever reason. There is nothing we can do. My parents tried, but they were shut down, pretty badly. I am sorry, Yung-Hong. We have to let it go...Look, we have Gray-Gray to take care of."

I made three cups of milk from evaporated milk powder and put out three plates. Two had black sesame cakes; one had a slice of toasted bun. I soaked the bun in milk and pushed it in front of Gray-Gray. I could hear Gray-Gray smacking her lips as she enjoyed the bun. Yung-Hong did not care about the milk, which to me was a luxury. My parents diligently obtained powdered milk from the Dong Bei Province so their two daughters would have the protein and calcium they needed. Both of us had passed the age to receive the one-pound milk quota for babies and toddlers. But Yung-Hong loved the black sesame cake, just as I expected. She devoured it in no time.

"Black sesame will make your hair darker and shinier. So does milk," I said.

"Really? OK, then I will start drinking milk. They deliver it to my house every week. I do not like the taste. But I will try now." She started sipping the milk. "Your mom's so good. I've never had cakes like this. Yum!"

"She makes a batch every week. She said she will make one for you from now on."

"Really? Thank you. So you told her about me."

"Of course. She said you can come by anytime and join us for dinner, if your parents allow."

There was that cloud again.

"What's wrong? Tell me."

"Nothing...Well, around dinnertime, I will know whether my parents will be home or not. I haven't seen my dad for weeks now. My mom comes home at night if I don't see her at dinnertime. But I often have fallen asleep. I sometimes remember her tucking me in, but in the morning, she is gone again."

"But she does come home every night, right?"

Yung-Hong gazed vacantly, "I think so. She holds me in bed sometimes while I sleep. But I am not sure." I saw tears creeping up her eyes.

"Well, you can certainly spend evenings with us if your parents are not going to be there. Ask your mom when you see her…No, I have an idea. Let's write her a note together."

So this was what we came up with:

> Dear Mama,
> I met a new friend, Morning Feather. She is really nice, and her family asks if I can have dinner with them when you are not going to be home for dinner. But if you are home, I will stay with you.
>
> I love you.
> Yung-Hong

This was my part:

> Dear Mrs. Liu,
> My name is Morning Feather, and I live in #9 Ding Yin Street. My mom asks if you will allow Yung-Hong to have dinner with us. Of course, my mom would be delighted if you and Officer Liu can come and join us as well whenever you have time.
>
> Sincerely,
> Morning Feather

Thursday after school, as I rushed to my door, I saw Yung-Hong waving a note to me excitedly.

"My mom said yes! She won't be home this evening."

"She won't be home, and you are happy?" I teased her, but I immediately realized that I should not have.

I quickly changed the topic and invited her to see the food my mom had started preparing—boiled eggs stewed with roast pork, sweet and sour cabbages, and glass noodles.

"Wow, superb! I guess you guys got eggs on the black market?"

"Yeah, but don't shout. We cannot use up our rice and flour quota, unlike most other families. So Mom used these ration coupons to exchange for eggs and meat."

"What about the glass noodles? I haven't seen them since I left Dong Bei Province."

"Ah, I think that's where they got them." *Must be Da-Ye (my dad's older brother) who "smuggled" them to us*, I thought. But I did not want to talk about that yet.

Yung-Hong fell in love with my mom even before she met her. So when Mom walked in the door from a busy day of work, Yung-Hong was especially keen on making Mom feel how helpful and pleasant a guest she was. While Mom cooked, we helped wash and chop vegetables and set up the dining area and dishes.

Soon Dad came home, and the room was filled with the fragrance of food and warmth and laughter. It was almost bedtime when Dad and I walked Yung-Hong home. Yung-Hong became our frequent dinner guest over the next few months. After pleading letters from Mrs. Liu, my mom started to accept eggs, apples, and even whole boxes of cooked dinner from Yung-Hong when she came over for dinner. Mom reworked the food items Yung-Hong brought and made them super scrumptious.

I could see that my cheeks were starting to plump up. Gray-Gray had been shedding her gray baby fur and gradually putting on a slick black coat. But the changes were more pronounced in Yung-Hong. Her hair was no longer yellow but now dark and shining, like jet stones. Her fair complexion became rosy pink. Most importantly, she became happy.

On one autumn night, the wind started to pick up. A few leaves dangled in the wind and twirled downward to bring hurried footsteps to our barely started dinner party. Mrs. Liu, in full military uniform, stood by our door. Yung-Hong jumped in her seat. Despite her obvious gratitude to my family, Mrs. Liu seemed to have no time for pleasantries.

"Yung-Hong, you have to come with me quickly," she said in an anxious tone.

Yung-Hong's look reminded me of Gray-Gray hiding in the trash can. She came to hug me. Her arms locked so tightly that I lost my train of thought. An overwhelming sadness permeated my body from her. I could not comprehend it. But Yung-Hong seemed to know what was happening. She choked as she was being dragged away with Gray-Gray in her hands.

"I will take good care of Gray-Gray. I will always remember you. Please don't forget me..." Her words lingered in the chilly wind.

That night, a long, shrieking cat's meow woke me up. I asked my parents if I could go outside to see if it was Gray-Gray. Both said no, just as all of a sudden, there seemed to be many cats shrieking and running outside.

I fell half asleep. In my dreams, I could see Gray-Gray's jet-black eyes hauntingly turn into Yung-Hong's eyes.

Once again, I was woken up by heart-piercing shrieks. The morning sunlight blinded me as I ran toward the sound. I saw Gray-Gray struggling in my neighbor Uncle Su's hands at the door-way by the street.

My heart sank, but I ran after them. Before I could stop him, Uncle Su threw Gray-Gray onto a passing truck carrying red bricks.

"No!" I kept running after Gray-Gray. But the truck was fast and quickly became distant. Gray-Gray's meowing faded as her gray figure against the red bricks became a blur in my eyes. I seemed to hear her cry, "I will always remember you. Please don't forget me..."

CHAPTER 3

THE POPCORN MAN

I sat in the blazing sun, ten cents in one hand, a bowl of corn in the other, waiting for the popcorn man. He promised he would be here. It was my nap time on this unseasonably hot autumn afternoon. I could have waited in the house. But I didn't want to miss him, because finally I had corn.

Normally on Sundays, he woke me up with the popping sound. I would run out as quickly as I could to ask him to wait for me. Then, I ran back in to get a small bowl of rice and five cents from my parents. He said I was the only one who asked him to pop rice, and that was the reason he only charged me five cents. It took longer to pop corn kernels than rice.

I remember the first time he showed up in the neighborhood, I followed the fragrant smell and found him pouring gold and white fluffy popped corn into Xiao Liang's big bowl. Xiao Liang (Little Liang) let me taste it—it was crispy and naturally sweet. I asked for seconds.

Xiao Liang was Granny Liang's youngest son. The whole family lived in the three rooms on the south side of our courtyard. They were Muslims, of Hui ethnicity.

For some reason in the Chinese culture, Xiao Liang was called the "oldest son" (Lao Er Zi) by his parents. His older sister quit middle school and took over Granny Liang's position at a textile factory, starting as an apprentice. His older brother quit middle school and drove platform carts together with his dad.

As I called Granny Liang "granny," her children were considered a generation ahead of me. It was fine calling his brother and sister my uncle and auntie, but there was no way I would call Xiao Liang my uncle. He was only a few years older and thin as a stick.

Xiao Liang was nice enough to push a couple more pieces of popcorn into my hands before he warned, "That's it, no more," and walked home.

I was left with him, the popcorn man.

"You have corns to pop?" he asked. I was taken aback when my eyes fell on his face—it was a half-blackened face, with one of his eyes glassy looking and the other one, dirty and embedded with rocks.

My reaction saddened him. He looked down to the popping machine, which was a metal heating pot connected to a huge leather bag. I looked at the machine, too, thinking that might be the culprit for his ruined face.

"No, it is not the popper." He seemed to know what I was thinking. "It was a factory explosion. I was only seventeen then. I had very little disability benefits. So I've been popping corn for ten years now."

He was only twenty-seven? He looked so old, way older than my parents or even Grandpa Liang.

"I am sorry. We don't have corn at home," I said shyly, draping my hands along my sides to show proper manners, which I learned at school, when addressing an elder.

"You can pop rice if you want," he said encouragingly, and I was delighted.

He opened up the pot cover and carefully poured the small bowl of rice in. I noticed his hands shaking almost uncontrollably as he worked. But I also noticed that his hands were unexpectedly clean and fair colored. He started to rotate the handle so that the pot turned over the open fire.

"Ready or not, here it comes…" As he was saying it, a big loud bang shook the ground, and I closed my eyes and covered my ears subconsciously.

Popped rice did not taste nearly as good as popcorn, but I enjoyed it. But popped rice got old pretty quickly after a few weeks. Yet I could not stop popping rice, because I was afraid that the popcorn man would not come back if I stopped. No one else in the neighborhood was a consistent customer.

I started to beg my parents for corn. It was not something readily available. The regular market only had quota food, which consisted of rice, flour, bleached flour, and corn flour. The black market didn't have it, either—who would want to buy whole corn? Finally, my dad went to the black market and asked a farmer whether he could bring some corn for us that Sunday. The farmer said yes. I eagerly told the popcorn man as he was making, hopefully, the last popped rice for me.

"That's great." He turned to me to respond, and his towel fell from his right shoulder. I leaned over, trying to catch it, but it dangled in midair. Tracing it up, I saw that the towel was button looped onto his shirt.

Even though it was very hard to detect it from his blackened face, I noticed him blushing as he folded the towel carefully on his shoulder again. "The chicken lady stitched the button and the loop for me. She knows that I like to keep my hands clean." He became even more embarrassed as he found himself explaining to a seven-year-old.

I listened and nodded. "She is really smart."

"Yes, she is." The popcorn man became excited. "She breeds these black chickens, and both the chickens and the eggs sell a lot more than the regular kind in the black market." I remembered my mother buying these to help my aunt recover from her illness.

The popcorn man continued, "I help her round up the chickens. My face is ruined, but my legs work fine. She does not walk very well. Maybe she will take me someday." He looked at me tentatively. "Then maybe I don't have to pop corn anymore."

However, I made him promise to come back the following week, because I would have corn. He agreed.

⇥⊹ ⊹⇤

I finally stood up. The sun was slanting to the west, taking on an orange tint. I thought about being happy for the popcorn man as I looked at my sweaty ten cents and the bowl of corn. *Maybe I should go look for black chickens at the black market. Would I see him there?*

CHAPTER 4

SILKWORMS AND LASSOS

S ome say time heals all wounds. In a child's ever-growing mind, new things often come in to replace the old. But would memories truly fade, or were they just pushed into the back of the mind, where they waited to resurface again? When Yung-Hong and Gray-Gray were gone, a part of my world fell apart. I went about the same routine as usual, yet I constantly looked up and around, hoping I could catch a glimpse of them again somewhere in the corner of my eyes. When the popcorn man stopped coming into my neighborhood, I had decided that I should be happy for him. Maybe the reason he stopped coming was a good one. Maybe someone whom he loved and someone who loved him happily detained him.

To nurse my wounds, I welcomed all the distractions outside of my routine. The first field trip of second grade in the spring was a tour of the silk farm, southeast of Beijing. The tour guide and farm coordinator took us into the reception area and pointed at a gigantic silk screen filling a whole wall of the big room. It must have been forty feet wide and twelve feet tall. On the off-white background, red peonies, yellow chrysanthemums, pink roses, and orange lilies drooped their opulence. The rich sheen made them look real, with an almost watery translucence, while the bluebirds and cardinals seemed to jump off the screen.

"This screen is made completely from silk and completely from the silk produced on this farm." Everyone applauded.

The silk farm coordinator led us into the "nursery" first. Second graders were not a quiet group. However, the minute we stepped into the nursery, a rhythmic concert overpowered our chatter. They were the crunching sounds of the silkworms feeding on mulberry leaves. My eyes fell onto rows of trays extending from one end of the room to the other. All of a sudden, I saw the dances—thousands of white or ivory-colored silkworms moved among green leaves on these trays.

They might be small individually, but the sheer number of them and their constant movements seemed massive to me.

"We should call this the 'Warm Worm Room,' not a nursery." I said to Min-Min, who was wiping her sweat. It was a good thing that we did not stay there too long. Many of us were starting to get uncomfortable in our early spring warm clothes.

We stopped next at the silk extraction room or "the factory." Big monster machines filled the room, two in a row. Each machine had a big reel across the top and a long, tank-like bottom coming up to waist height. I could not see what was inside these tanks, but steam shot up from there. A few young women walked along these machines and sometimes pulled something from under the steam up to the grooves of the reels. As my eyes adjusted to the intricate dances of light, I was able to detect that these women were pulling strands of silk, twisting them together into a thread and then reeling them through on top.

We then arrived at the silk dying and weaving room. A splendid red silk sheet caught my eyes immediately. It was being woven together with gold threads. The shuttles dashed back and forth, and I thought to myself, *I could wear it as a shawl to the most extravagant party or maybe make it into a Qi-Pao* (a figure hugging traditional Chinese dress from the Qing Dynasty). However, the coordinator never stopped long enough for me to savor the moment. As she led us out of the weaving room, she said that silk weaving was a very minor part of the silk farm. Most of the revenue came from selling raw silk produced by the reeling process we saw before.

Finally, we sat down in a dark room next to the reception area. The coordinator pointed at the pictures on the walls and explained the life cycle of the silkworm. Then she picked up a few pieces of brown paper from the baskets in the front. "These are the eggs of the silkworms," she said as she pointed at the paper. I could see tiny little black dots on it.

"We are asking for your help. As part of the education program, we ask you to help the silkworms complete their life cycle. You have seen that in order for us to extract silk, silkworms die in the process and cannot complete nature's intended journeys for them. As farmers, we do realize the sadness in this process as we try to make a living ourselves. But you can do something good. Please take these eggs with you, care for them as they grow, and bring their eggs back here. You would preserve their life cycle; you would help them fulfill life's meaning. Would you help? Anyone?"

Her voice sounded like the dancing silk, lofty, elegant, and evocative. I looked around. All of the children were quiet, with their heads low.

"Min-Min, you have a mulberry tree in your yard, right?"

"No, I don't. That's Qu Bo's (Senior Uncle Qu) next door. He is a colonel."

"Same difference…Here," I grabbed Min-Min's hand and raised both of ours up. "We will help!" I called out. Min-Min pulled her hand away and gave me a nudge.

"You will," she said, and then she sighed. "Fine, me too."

The coordinator was very happy; our teacher was, too. So Min-Min and I took home a piece of palm-sized brown paper with twenty-eight silkworm eggs on it. We laid the paper in a shoe-box lid at my home and watched. I kept hoping a worm would hatch from an egg and come out. But there were still twenty-eight eggs after we patiently stared at them for a long time.

"So let's go get some mulberry leaves," I said.

"OK…" Min-Min raised one eyebrow but did not say anything.

I found out why when we were inside her yard—no trees. Dangling over the wall, a few mulberry leaves swayed. *Yes, she had told me before.*

"Don't worry. That's easy," I said, smiling. "You have a ladder?"

We brought one from her house and leaned it against the wall. I climbed up and grabbed a few leaves. I took one step down, but curiosity stopped me. My eyes were just above the wall, looking into Qu Bo's yard.

The yard was nicely tiled in slates. The mulberry tree on the far side provided almost complete shade for the yard and made it look solemn and somewhat mysterious. Now I started to understand Min-Min's hesitations. Qu Bo was a strange person on the block. He lived alone and seldom talked to anyone. As my parents were teachers, and they were always nice to people, they commanded a certain respect from all the neighbors. But whenever Qu Bo and my parents met on the street, Qu Bo barely nodded and never spoke. I remember my dad said Qu Bo was a retired colonel, and he had seen battles and wars and endured the hardest things in life.

However, there was no time to waste thinking about things. We ran back to my house and laid the leaves under the egg paper.

Still no worms.

I was having breakfast when I saw him, tumbling down the brown paper and onto the mulberry leaves.

"Min-Min!" I shouted loud enough for her to hear me from halfway down the block. "Mommy, Daddy, my first silkworm!"

He was so tiny, like a slimmer version of a black ant, but he had a lot of vigor. There were already holes in the leaf under him, and he found an edge and persistently chipped away.

"Go find Min-Min. Your silkworm will be here waiting for you, I promise," Mom said.

I ran and fetched Min-Min, and we did not leave the site until we had to run to beat the school's opening bell. Then in the afternoon, we ran all the way home as soon as school closed.

It was still him, alone, moving about the mulberry leaves.

"Min-Min, look at his eyes." They looked like little beads on his forehead.

"Beadie..." I murmured.

"That sounds like a good name," Min-Min said. So that was settled. We named him Beadie.

By the time Min-Min left for dinner, Beadie had a few new friends. When I saw Min-Min again the next morning, she was very excited that all the silkworms had hatched.

In the afternoon, I did the first cleaning of their droplets.

"You know people think these are precious things. They use them for pillows." Min-Min watched me dusting these droplets onto a piece of paper.

"I know," I said as I dumped them into the trash. "I had a silk-worm secretion pillow when I was a baby; so did my sister. Let's go get more leaves."

As the silkworms grew day by day, their colors turned from black to brown to white. They started to consume more than just a few leaves a day. And I started to have some difficulties getting the leaves from the ladder, as I had harvested almost all the low-hanging ones.

Beadie was still the biggest and strongest of them all. He con-stantly raised two thirds of his body and moved around vigorously. And he ate with gusto. Min-Min and I often took him outside of the shoe-box lid and put him on a single leaf to watch. He seemed to know that we were watching and moved his head left and right as he fed. Sometimes, he would cut through in the middle of a leaf to feed, but he always turned back just before breaking the leaf in half. We had never seen other silkworms do that. They always tackled the edges. We thought Beadie knew that he was our pet and was performing tricks for us.

On a very hot afternoon, I kept sweating as I tried reaching for the leaves from the top of the ladder. No luck. There was no way I could get any of them from there. It had been almost twenty days since I started fetching leaves on this ladder, and I would always look into Qu Bo's yard—always empty, always shady, like it was deserted. I knew that today I had to get up to the roof, Qu Bo's roof, to get to the leaves. I swung my legs over the wall and walked on all fours to the sloped roof of Qu Bo's house. I tested the stability of a few roof tiles and climbed up.

As long as my hands were still on the roof, I did not feel scared at all. But now I had to stand up to reach for the leaves. I tried, and a few tiles made scratching sounds. So I bent down and readjusted the positions of my feet and reached up again.

"What are you doing on my roof?" A thunderous voice made me lose my balance, and I slid off the incline.

"Oh God!" I could not decide whether to keep my eyes open or shut, and I desperately grabbed onto the tiles.

But the tiles and I were still slipping fast.

I guessed I finally stopped. I saw my hands holding on to a couple of loose tiles. And my legs were…*Where were they? Ah, in midair. Where were the supports then?* I found one where my stomach was. My stomach was exactly where the ledge was, kind of painful. But the most important support was around my ankles—two strong hands locked onto them tightly.

"It's not very far from the ground. I will change hands to your waist." Qu Bo held my waist and carried me down to the ground. And then Qu Bo himself jumped down from the bench built under the eave, exactly where I was falling off.

"I am very sorry," I said.

"You should be." He scolded me, "Which family's girl would do such a thing? Going onto another's roof? Do you not have any rules?"

"I am very sorry. We have a school project to raise silkworms. The only mulberry tree is in your yard. I had to…"

"No, you don't. Don't you ever come onto my roof again. You hear me?"

"But what do I feed the silkworms?"

"None of my business." He walked toward his door with his hands behind his back. My apology and gratitude were quickly fading.

"Please, help me; my silkworms will die…" I pleaded.

"I told you not to bother me. Leave now. I am going to lock the door."

I was very upset; I had no option but to leave.

The white and ivory-colored silkworms greeted us with eager movements. But I had nothing to offer them. I could not settle down that evening. I pounced and agitated. Anxiety was gnawing me alive every time I looked at my silkworms. There had to be another way. I found a street map and started to study it.

I arranged with Min-Min the next day to look for mulberry leaves in the neighborhood. We set out immediately after school and searched street by street until nightfall. We were tired, hungry, and completely defeated. There were no other mulberry trees within a mile's radius. I sent Min-Min home and apologized for keeping her out for so long. I then turned to Qu Bo's door. I knocked, quietly at first and then not so quietly. Finally, I realized that Qu Bo would not open his door for me.

Beadie was waiting for me. He raised up his front body with efforts to see me. Other silkworms were quieter and did not move much, maybe to preserve energy. I had failed them.

I had never asked my parents to help me with other people before. That night I asked my mom. She said she would go talk to Qu Bo in the morning.

The next morning Mom came back and said Qu Bo did not open his door, and she would try again in the evening.

When Min-Min and I got home that afternoon, Beadie was not moving. I gently touched his head. His eyes were no longer clear and shiny. I cursed under my lips and gave Beadie a determined look before I took a confused Min-Min to her place. I was going to get up on that roof again, but I was shocked when I looked above where we normally leaned the ladder—barbwires—they were newly laid on top of the wall.

That was it. That meant war!

I stood there watching the barbwires. All of a sudden, I saw things with such clarity. It became a single vision.

I must have the mulberry leaves.

"Min-Min, I will be right back." I ran home, dug into my treasure cove, and took out the jar with my marble collection—almost four hundred of them now, many rare ones. I had been collecting and trading marbles for as long as I could remember. Most of them were made of glass in diameters of either ten or twenty millimeters. The clear glass ones each had a different color design inside and out. Depending on the design, they would fetch different prices. Then there were the colored glass ones, granite or gemstone ones. They themselves were already rare regardless of the design.

I went to Uncle Su's house across from mine and asked for his son, Tong. Tong used to be a timid child when we still played together in kindergarten. But eventually he turned into a bully. Because of our early friendship, we avoided each other's path as we grew—a courtesy we afforded to each other.

"What do you want?" Tong was eyeing my marble jar already.

"Some help, making lassos."

"Then this would be mine?" He reached over for the jar, and I let go.

⊨⊹⊹⊨

I climbed up the ladder again. I swung the lasso, and it landed on a branch. I pulled it. The branch swung back. I swung the lasso again. This time, it grabbed hold of a large branch, and I pulled it firmly toward me. Leaves floated down, and Min-Min caught them and set them in a shoe box. I did it again. A branch snapped…A squeak of the door…I did not even look down. I swung my lasso again.

"Do you not understand respect?" Qu Bo, standing on the far side of the courtyard, demanded.

33

"Do you not understand helping others?" I shot back.

"Helping others? I am helping you. You are out of line. I am straightening you out!" he exclaimed.

"And you are cruel. You'd rather let my silkworms die than let me take a few mulberry leaves from your yard."

"It is *my* yard. And you have no right to take anything."

"Last time I checked, the land belongs to the government; your house belongs to the government and the mulberry tree, as well as all the trees in China, belongs to the public! I have as much right to them as you do!"

He narrowed his eyes. The bantering annoyed him.

"I know your parents. Maybe I should have a talk with them. It is a small wonder that they could produce a child like you."

The mentioning of my parents upset me. I started to shout at the top of my lungs.

"Go ahead and talk to my parents and tell them about your cruelty! You'd rather hurt the silkworms! You'd hurt me and my school project! And what kind of animal are you to put up barb-wires to prevent a child from preserving silkworms' life cycle!"

As I shouted, I violently swung the lasso and pulled the branches and leaves. My feverish and drastic movements landed my arm several times on the barbwires.

I could also feel his anger rising like a fire. But strangely, when the words came out of his mouth, they were cold and steely.

"You need to learn to stop before you hurt yourself or, even worse, hurt others. Mark my words; I will teach you a lesson. You shall be taught a lesson." Then, just like that, he went back to his house.

I climbed down the ladder, panting.

"See, we have way too many." Min-Min handed me, not the shoe box, but a big utility crate full of mulberry leaves. I stretched out my arms to receive it, but her eyes widened at my right arm, and she pulled back her hands with the crate.

"You are bleeding!" she gasped.

I looked to where she was staring at—three deep scrapes from my elbow to forearm and a few punch wounds. Blood oozed out and dripped down. I felt like something exploded in my head and then it went dark in front of my eyes. I fell to the ground.

"Ouch." That hurt my butt really badly and kept me conscious.

"Are you OK?" Min-Min supported me on my left side.

"OK, I think." I did not immediately open my eyes.

I must stand up. I need to go feed the silkworms. I said to myself.

I opened my eyes and tentatively looked at my right arm again. It made me queasy, but I did not faint. I took a deep breath and got to my feet.

"Min-Min, I need to go feed the silkworms. Can you handle the cleanup here?"

"No problem." She handed me the crate, her eyes full of worry.

I ran.

I lay down the freshest leaf on the table and put Beadie on it. He just lay there.

Then I put a dozen leaves into the shoe box. The silkworms danced in frenzy. I could hear the eagerness in each bite.

When Min-Min came, I was washing my arm in a basin of clean water. Blood turned the water pink.

"Morning Feather, Beadie's not eating." Min-Min hunched in front of the table.

Big drops of tears fell into the basin, mixing with my blood.

Min-Min helped put peroxide on my wounds and wrapped my arm in bandages. "I was worried about you," she said. "You shouted like a crazy person. I have never seen you like that. You were like on fire. I was scared." That brought tears to my eyes again, but I did not let them fall.

"I am sorry. I am really sorry." I let out these words as if pleading, and I felt exhausted. I could not take it any longer. I needed to sleep. "I will see you tomorrow." I half heard Min-Min closing the door as she left.

Beadie died the next morning.

I did not move for a long time. I no longer had tears. I had hate.

If Min-Min was scared before, she was terrified of me now. She was afraid to say anything that might send me over the edge.

After school, I took the utility crate and stomped into her yard. I set up the ladders with loud bangs and stormed up with lassos in hand.

But the yard was empty. There was no sound and no one in sight.

I stood there, lost.

I managed to get enough leaves and helped clean up. I left in a daze. I fed the silkworms and had to go to bed again. I felt screwed up in my head. I could not distinguish whether I was sleeping or awake.

But something was different in the morning. A silkworm wrapped herself in a few strands of silk. The sight of it made my heart jump. I carefully watched. She spat a figure eight around her body, translucent, shimmery. With every movement, she sent a splatter of happiness into my poisoned heart...

Life is the best cure of any pain, I learned from that moment. Whatever happened seemed so insignificant compared to the preparation of a new life and many new beginnings. I laid down layers of brown paper in the shoe box and carefully moved the remaining silkworms into it, not disrupting the one cocooning in the shoe-box lid. Each piece of brown paper, I imagined, would be gradually pulled away as the eggs were laid on top, revealing a fresh one underneath.

By evening, almost all the silkworms started spinning silk, each finding a wedge between the sidewall of the shoe box and the bottom. They showed so much dedication, making the figure-eight movements. Nothing else mattered. When I woke up in the morning, they were all peacefully asleep inside their cocoons. I took the one in the lid and reunited her with her other friends. I breathed a sigh of relief, knowing they would sleep for quite a few days. There would be nothing required of me except for keeping them safe.

Before long, I started to worry again. Now I had twenty-seven cocoons. I had never worried about the gender of the silkworms until now. Even in the most fortunate situations, all my silkworms would pair up except one (I did not learn that male silkworms wander until many years later)! This wariness put me back into the staring game. I watched the cocoons intensely. They were colorful, mostly quite light. But I watched them so much that I believed silk was naturally colorful, not dyed. From then on, every time I saw colorful silk garments, I imagined silkworms spinning colorful cocoons.

I was woken up by fluttering of wings. I took a flashlight and went to the shoe box, where three pairs of moths fluttered about in curvy movements, each pair's tails joining. They were of tan or brown color, with slightly smaller wings and slightly fatter bodies than the quarter-sized moth we often saw in Beijing. I yawned and went back to bed.

During the day while I was at school, most of the silkworms finished their metamorphosis and mated. When I came home, quite a few of the moths had laid eggs and died. I removed a sheet of paper full of eggs, making sure not to disturb the ones mating. I counted, only twenty minutes of mating, followed by about an hour to lay eggs, and then death. It seemed incredibly short, compared to other life forms, even compared to their own lives.

I looked at the last three cocoons uneasily. If life was worth living for the briefest final moment of happiness and the giving of life, then not being able to fulfill it would be so devastating. I wanted to say a prayer.

"Mommy!" I shouted in the dark and turned on the ceiling light, dropping my flashlight on the table with a clunk. Both Mom and Dad raised their heads but shielded their eyes.

"Morning Feather, what's the matter?" they asked simultaneously.

"Come over here." I dragged Dad over. Mom followed.

"Ha, interesting!" Dad caught on first. "What do you make of that?" He turned to mom.

Mom looked carefully and, with a smile, said, "Life finds a way."

Three moths were joining their tails together in a three-way dance. Their wings raised and settled, making the most beautiful snowflake like shapes, but brown in color. I could almost hear their songs.

There were 1620 eggs; I counted them many times.

My teacher arranged a ride for me after school to send the eggs back to the farm. Min-Min had a recital that day. So I went alone.

I found the coordinator in the room next to the reception area where she had so eloquently persuaded me to take on the silkworm eggs. I proudly handed her the sheets of paper.

"Sixteen hundred twenty eggs. I counted them."

"Congratulations, you've done a wonderful thing for these silk-worms." She accepted them gratefully.

"What happens now?" I asked.

"Let's see," she said as she looked at her logbook, "you took twenty-eight eggs. We keep some more as seeds, for students like you who are willing to help the silkworms fulfill their life cycles. The rest of them go to production," she said matter of factly.

"Production? You mean the babies of my silkworms will go through…" I pointed to the factory.

"Yes." She picked up a pair of scissors and cut a small part of the paper. The cutting sound so foreign.

"Roughly forty eggs from each paper," she said and smiled back at me, and then she noticed my shock.

"I know it is hard to understand." Her voice softened. "You probably spent a lot of time and effort with these silkworms. But this is the nature of the silk business. People depend on it—families to feed." She dropped the small pieces of paper into the basket by the wall and stashed the larger pieces in the drawer.

"Now go home and be happy about your good deed."

I started walking, but the images of my silkworms in the shoe-box lids were jumbled up with the silkworms in the trays and the steam of the reeling machines.

I almost reached door and realized I had another box in my hand.

"Here," I raised the opened box to her. "I brought these back, too."

"The cocoons?"

I had arranged the cocoons neatly in the box: nine white, six ivory, five yellow, three pink, three peach, and one green.

She came around the table and looked at me with disbelief. "You are so...careful." She inspected the cocoons and then me.

"Student Morning Feather, may I ask for these?"

I nodded.

She studied me more intently. "Student Morning Feather, I am asking for the cocoons for myself, not on behalf of the farm."

I nodded again.

"I have a daughter who is a little older than you. How old are you?"

"Eight."

"She's eleven. She and I knit silk from the cocoons that the silkworms come out of, like the ones you have. But we don't have a lot. We would appreciate you giving us yours."

I nodded one more time.

"Thank you." She smiled broadly and, as if remembering something, she turned around and brought out the small piece of paper from the basket.

41

"Want to do it again?"

"No!" I was surprise at how fast I replied.

She sighed and came around to put her hand on my shoulder, "My daughter and I thank you. With your cocoons added, she will have enough for a vest for winter now." Her voice again became silky and tantalizing.

But I felt the world was beyond my comprehension.

The silkworm story might end here, as I commanded the memory to fade into the background and be replaced by other stories of childhood.

But another person would once again bring it back in time— Qu Bo had not forgotten about it, and neither would he let me.

CHAPTER 5

TUTORING AND AN OFFER OF MARRIAGE

My childhood life was quite simple, as far as I can recall. My family was my sanctuary, and I paid attention to only the things I cared about (for the most part, that was acquiring knowledge) or the things I was required to do by my parents and authoritative figures, and I ignored pretty much everything else.

Tutoring became one of the requirements for me when we first entered third grade, around 1978. A few years after the downing of the "Gang of Four," there seemed to be a new movement of promoting learning and increasing education effectiveness. I believe that was also when colleges started to pop up, and my parents secretly taught night schools.

The big movement trickled down into our small classroom of forty. The top five academically ranked students were paired up as tutors with the bottom five. As I ranked number one, I was paired with number forty—Ray. He always sat in the middle of the last row of the class. I remembered I could often hear his gruff voice joking and laughing in the back, not paying attention to the teacher. No wander he was failing.

I was very upset that I got moved from my first-row seat to the desk next to him so that I could keep an eye on him during class. However, it was the teacher's decision, and I could not say no. My assignment would be doing homework with him together after school and tutoring him as needed.

The last row was at least twenty feet away from the teacher's podium. I was often annoyed that I could hardly hear the teacher. If there was any chatter or distractions around me, I would be upset and cast cold looks at the source. So when Ray started one of his lame jokes with his pals, I turned to him with my icy stare. He seemed startled and lowered his eyes. I noticed that he had very long eyelashes, like the foreign movie stars we had seen on posters. Ray obediently returned to his books, and I felt victorious.

After a while, one of Ray's pals to my right side started some gossip about some girl. I got really agitated and was ready to show my displeasure. But Ray looked up at me and then crumbled a piece of paper into a ball and threw it onto his yapping pal's desk. The guy looked back at Ray. Ray smiled and gestured a stop sign.

After that, my surroundings were, for the most part, quiet and attentive.

I found Ray soft spoken and obedient, quite different from the rowdy and belligerent rascal that I had been hearing about. His home was a block away from mine, across from the grocery store. From the outside, it looked like a bump slapped onto the wall. Once inside, there was that slightly familiar structure: on the left, kitchen; on the right, bedroom/living room combo. Only his kitchen was more of an edge of that room with a stove, and the living room had one bed with a small square table on it. There was barely enough room between the bed and the window for one person to pass comfortably. I figured he and his parents probably all slept on that bed at night, temporarily placing the table sideways on the ground between the bed and the window.

The platform bed was quite high, and it took me a good jump to get up to the table. I could hear the traffic outside and even passersby talking and laughing while we did homework together. For every subject, I would be completely finished while Ray was still halfway. Then he would try to make conversation, and I would always say, with much authority, "No talking. Concentrate on your homework." And he would obey and try very hard to finish them quickly so we could compare answers. Then we would go over all the questions he did wrong until he understood why. After that, I would go home to play with my sister and wait for my mom to return. To me, the quicker we finished, the better off we were. I always felt the low ceiling of Ray's house pressing down on me.

After the first week, Ray's quiz results came back. Both his math and reading were in the low seventies; science was sixty-nine. That meant all his scores had improved from failing. He was in a particularly good mood that day.

"Can we take a five-minute break between subjects today?" Ray asked, and I agreed. We did math first and checked the answers. "Wait here." He jumped off the bed and ran to the kitchen side. Then he seemed to be digging into the ceiling, and I heard the clattering of glass jars. When he came back, he handed me two saltine crackers.

"Not on the table." I did not want crumbs on my homework. I jumped off and perched on the windowsill, one cracker in each hand. "And you?" I asked him, noticing he was empty handed now.

"Nah, I don't want any." I put one in his hand. He smiled and said, "Water," and brought two glasses of water and set them on the windowsill.

I ate my cracker slowly, mesmerized by the setting sun, orange melting into blue. Somehow, the tiny house no longer seemed depressive, but rather cozy.

"We need to set a goal for you. Each week you need to move up five points on all subjects." I drank the last of my water.

"Then I'd be catching up with you soon."

"That'd be the ultimate goal," I said and tried to climb up the bed. Ray was so fast that his one hand was under my arm while the other was setting down the glass. And then his spare hand came under my other arm, and he hoisted me onto the bed. He climbed up himself and went to the other side of the table. We resumed homework.

The quiz results were often distributed on Tuesday after recess. During my regular walk around the school field during recess the following Tuesday, my uncooperative braids loosened. I rushed to the classroom to fix them.

During those years, the only two acceptable hairstyles for school were either the short-bob hairstyle or braids. When I was younger, Mom always braided my hair. She separated my hair into two sides and braided each tightly until I felt my scalp was pulled back and tears were nearly welling up my eyes. Only tightly braided hair could last the whole day of my active routine.

When I started school, I had learned to braid my own hair. The problem was, I could never braid them as tightly as Mom did. On occasion, I had to rush somewhere quiet to fix my hair.

I figured that as everybody was at recess, my classroom would be private enough for me to battle with my braids. I sat down in the back, pulled the rubber bands off from both sides, and let the hair loose. Then I separated the two sides and tied the left with a rubber band for later. I proceeded to work on the braid on the right, making three strands of hair intertwining one another. Finally, I came to the bottom where I needed to tie up the ends. Holding the three strands of hair forming the braid with my left hand, I used my right hand to grab the rubber band on the desk and started to twirl it around onto the end of my braid. But my thick, slick hair slipped from my hands and the rubber band. The braided strands unraveled like springs releasing themselves. I let out a frustrated groan.

"Can I help you?" A low voice coming from the back door startled me. I turned and found Ray, not even four feet away, leaning against the wall next to the door.

Shock and embarrassment overwhelmed me, and for a moment, I did not respond.

"How long have you been standing there?" I was not sure why I asked, but I did.

"A while. I was nervous about the quiz results, so I thought I'd come here and sit at my desk." His answer seemed to calm me.

Ray walked over to my desk. "I will help you hold your braid next time, and you can put the rubber band on," he said softly.

"OK, thank you." I had to admit I needed help. The class would be coming back soon, and I needed my hair up in braids. So I raised my hands to start and felt Ray's hand stopping me.

"You know the movie stars now let their hair loose?" he asked me. I was in a desperate panic that I did not understand. Ray continued, "I can see why." He let go of my hands so that I could start braiding.

I was so relieved that we were able to finish my braids in one try, because the bell sounded right after, indicating that recess had ended.

Ray reached the goal that week. Now all three subjects were in the high 70s from the weekly quiz. We were chatting excitedly on the way home together that day. A friend of his wanted to do something together with him, but he declined. For a second I thought to myself how unlikely it was that I walked home with Ray under normal circumstances, but I chased the thought away.

We just started math homework, and a truck stopped outside. His father came in and did not look at me, but he said to him, "Ray, we need you to work."

"Dad…" Ray went out for a moment and came back.

"I am sorry, but I have to work. Please go home."

I did not say anything. I picked up my things and walked to the door.

"I will make it up," he said behind me.

The next day he did not show up at school until noon. He looked tired and sleepy. When he finally came, he hunched over his desk the whole afternoon. On the way home, he told me that he did not go to bed until early morning.

"Hey, Ray, you owe me one, you son of a bitch," called a teenage boy on a bicycle as he passed by.

"Yeah, buddy, I won't forget." Ray waved to him and accented himself with a gruff voice, definitely not the kind I had become accustomed to. What shocked me was when we arrived at his home, that is, if I could still make it out. From floor to treetop height, covering the whole front of the house, were neatly stacked red bricks.

"Once we finish building out the house, I will have my own room," he said proudly.

The doorway was still clear, but the window was almost completely blocked. We turned on the lights when we got in. As we proceeded to start homework, I noticed his right hand was wrapped with a handkerchief. Bloodstains were visible.

"What happened?"

"What? Oh, this? It is nothing. A couple of bricks fell. Let's get to work."

Work seemed much harder that day for Ray, as he had missed both math and reading classes. And he was clearly tired.

Despite the missed classes and sleep, Ray's third weekly quizzes returned an eighty-two on math, seventy-nine on reading, and seventy-eight on science. I breathed a sigh of relief that Tuesday and made special efforts to reinforce the past week's contents.

He seemed sheepish. "I did not raise five points this week."

"But you raised four, one, and two," I encouraged him. "Next week is midterms; prepare well, and we have the national holiday in between, I want you to reach eighty-five."

"I will, I promise." He looked at me for a long time, one hand holding his head.

"What?" I asked.

"Promise that you won't get mad if I tell you."

I shrugged. *Do I want to know?* I thought to myself. But curiosity got the better of me. "Fine, I promise."

He bit his lips and stuttered. Now I remembered he often stuttered in front of me. "Would you marry me if I reach eighty-five on the exams?"

"No." I shot back a quick answer and shrugged again. I knew I was not mad. But I certainly wasn't prepared for this kind of question.

"How high do I need to score so that you will agree to marry me?"

I fell into the trap of this question and answered, "See, I almost always get one hundred. Anyone who ever thinks about marrying me should get at least ninety-five. Besides, I am nine years old. You are like what, ten?"

"I will be eleven in November."

"Whatever. It will be at least ten, twenty years before we should even consider such a thing." I started to put on my coat. The blockage of the window made me lose track of time. I was afraid that I was really late.

"So if I get ninety-five on all the exams...and...and if I am twenty-eight and you are twenty-six, you will agree to marry me?"

"I got to go." And I ran out.

It was really late. The last burgundy from the sun was drowning in darkness. I felt a chill as the wind brushed harshly against my face and neck when I picked up the pace.

"Morning Feather," Ray called from behind.

"I am late," I shouted without slowing down. His footsteps caught up with mine.

"You forgot this," Ray said running alongside me and wrapped my scarf around my neck.

"Thanks." I did not stop and did not look back.

I was sick the following day, apparently having caught cold the evening before. I missed school. Then the four-day national-holiday weekend came. I recovered and studied.

The following Monday was midterm for math; Tuesday, reading; Wednesday, science. When the results were published on Thursday, I was mildly interested in how Ray fared—in the seventies on all subjects.

The head teacher declared tutoring a huge success as all five tutored students had improved their scores and their rankings. He also declared tutoring over because with the new ranking, it was hard to figure out who should be tutored now.

However, the expected relief did not come to me. It seemed that the rowdy or the gossipy groups, who used to ignore my existence as I ignored theirs, shot me glances or giggled when I went by. As I walked home that afternoon, passing Ray and his gang, five or six of them, hanging around outside his home, they stopped and looked at me. One guy whispered something to Ray, and Ray laughed. I did not like their looks; I did not like Ray's laugh. But I ignored it as usual.

The next morning at recess, when I had just started taking my daily walk around the sports field, Chang-Fu sneaked up behind me. Him, I never liked. He was the kind of person who peddled information for personal gain. You could almost see that everything going on inside him immediately turned muddy.

"Word on the street is that you are betrothed to Ray." He eyed me slyly as he got onto to the topic after some unwelcome chitchatting.

I stopped and turned to face him slowly, but very decidedly, not only to face him but also the whole sports field.

"You listen carefully, Chang-Fu Wan," I began. I was just over four feet tall and barely sixty pounds, a slender girl who seemed not to be able to withstand the slightest breeze. But I had a voice that could carry, a coldness like ice that could chill the bones, and a sternness like blade that could cut stone.

"Whoever told you that lie can come and face me. I will show him what a liar and a cheat he is. If he dares to do so now, or whenever he can gather up his cowardliness, I will be ready for him." I glanced around the field, noticing at least half of the school was looking at me. And Ray and his gang were not even fifteen feet away.

"But if *you* are the one spreading these rumors," I narrowed my eyes, "say it now so everybody can hear you. Do you understand me?"

"Hey, hey, I was just, you know, thought you'd like to know…Just trying to be nice…Hey, consider it withdrawn, all right? Nothing said." Chang-Fu started to walk away but found himself in the path of Ray and his gang. He had to make an L rather embarrassingly.

I turned slowly to walk in the opposite direction, clenching my teeth hard so as not to let that tear fall down until it began to hurt badly. Luckily, I reached a fountain and pretended to get a drink of water. "Are you all right?" Min-Min, a girl who sometimes hung out with me, came to ask.

"Yes…Could we walk home together after school, please?"

That weekend turned out to be a so-called Indian summer. Mom and I decided to take advantage of the beautiful weather for a shopping spree. She wore a green gingham dress with a white sash and carried a light-green hard plastic-molded tote. A stalk of celery cheerfully dangled its tail outside the tote, while red tomatoes, white turnips, and green peppers huddled inside the tote but peeked through the perforations. I, walking alongside her, wore my favorite white-flowered blue dress with ruffled collars. A basket, originally rescued from the trash, was now skillfully painted burgundy by my father to resemble an article of heirloom stature. It was filled to the brim with pecan crisps and sticky rice sticks. It nestled comfortably in my arms. The two of us must have looked like people from the picture books.

As we walked and talked, I suddenly sensed a cold glance in my direction. I looked up, and my stomach churned. A group of men, topless with dirty pants working side by side, slapped wet concrete onto bricks and laid them onto the newly forming walls. Among them was Ray, who had already turned back to focus on his work. I could not help but realize the look he gave me was not of an eleven-year-old; it was that of an injured man. Before I could ignore it and move on with my life, I stole a look back. In that moment, I caught Ray's father handing him half a cigarette. Ray stared it for a second as if to make a decision but then put it in his mouth. The rim burned red. And the sweat on his shoulders glistened in the sun. I realized once again that the not-yet-eleven-year-old Ray, in the midst of men, was actually taller and better built.

It did not take a genius to know that the effect of tutoring would wear off before the year's end—all five tutored students returned to their bottom ranking. The problem at the time in China was not wealth, because everybody was poor. It was knowledge—the knowledge that knowledge had power, and knowledge held the key to the future. For two decades, intellectuals were oppressed. Many of them were tortured and thrown to the bottom of society. But secretly, they cherished their best property—their intellect—and used it to survive. They passed knowledge to their children in the hopes that they would thrive. The laborers, on the other hand, valued their labor, slogans, and propaganda, and they made choices for their children along the same lines. Any chance for a success of the social experiment of tutoring would have been to spark something inside these five students. But that attempt failed. However, it was only a matter of time, because change was in the air.

⚞ ⚟

One afternoon during my last year in high school, two years after we had moved to a teachers' complex faraway, I searched for a new bookstore called the Trend. The bookstore featured newly translated books from the United States and European countries. I was surprised that I came face-to-face with my old neighborhood grocery store, which had been converted into a bookstore. It was now freshly painted with lots of glass windows. The mirroring glass reflected a young man in a muscle shirt and cargo shorts holding and swaying a baby, a cigarette in his mouth. I knew that was Ray even before I turned around to look at his face. He did not recognize me. It was around three fifty on an afternoon in 1987. The government had started to massively lay off or furlough workers in manufacturing plants. I turned and stepped into the bookstore.

At least he is helping his wife take care of their child. Many guys don't even do that, I thought to myself.

CHAPTER 6

HOW TO KILL A CHICKEN

Before third grade was over, Mom had taught me to be in charge of my own laundry. I had only two pairs of pants—blue and military green, and two shirt jackets—military green and blue. It was necessary to get one set laundered each week so that they were ready for the next. I would use the one and only washbasin in the house (yes, the one I made tea with when I was four). I would fill it with water from the tap in the courtyard and wash one article at a time. After a few trial runs with Mom's supervision, I got it down and felt really good about being able to take care of myself.

It was a beautiful Sunday morning, not long after the Indian summer. I set up the washbasin in front of our apartment and put my still very new military-green pants in the water to soak. Then I pulled over a small stool to sit on, started to soap up, and rubbed one pant leg at a time on the washboard.

That year was a great harvest season. The two date trees in the courtyard yielded three basins of dates for each family. Ours were honey stewed and jarred on the windowsill. I could smell the stewing dates from Grandma Su's suites—a sweet, saturating scent that made your mouth water.

Then a big ruckus broke out of Uncle Su's apartment.

"Gaaa gaaa guug…"

"Hack, you stupid bird." Uncle Su kicked his door open, clenching the big, feathery animal in his hands.

Struggling and gurgling, the rooster freed one wing from Uncle Su's clutches and flapped the orange flame of his feathers. Uncle Su slapped its head and took control of the rooster again. Then he proceeded to tie the rooster onto his wood horse. The rooster's body and the wood horse formed an X shape, leaving the rooster's head and feet hanging from either side.

Uncle Su then put a metal bucket under the rooster's head. Without a moment's hesitation, he grabbed a butcher's knife and sliced the rooster's neck open.

I was motionless at the shock of the scene. ✳

"Slow bleeding yields the tenderest meat," Uncle Su proclaimed proudly, looking around the courtyard where almost all the neighbors were gawking in awe. "You will see." He wiped the bloody blade with a victorious smile. I did not know where to look: the icy shine of the blade, Uncle Su's twisted face, or the dripping blood.

"*Gaaaa…*" All of a sudden, the loudest croak of the rooster broke the silence, and the wood horse fell at the fierce struggle of the rooster. The bucket was knocked sideways, letting the rooster break out of the rope binding him.

Stumbling for a second, the rooster stood up; neck broken and fallen to the left, red-hot crown flapping up and down, he charged toward me!

I froze.

Time froze.

A stout chest, masculine legs, and firm claws performed the last warrior's charge.

The sliced-open neck, the fallen head, the flapping crown, and the furious eyes came straight at me.

Then I saw blood, gushing and dripping with each step, coming closer...

I jumped up, ran back to the house, and banged the door shut. I could see the rooster standing in my washbasin, right on top of my soapy green pants. Blood fell drip-drip onto the white soap bubbles. Then he fell. The big orange flame half submerged into the green-and-white-tinted water, like a snow lotus, the rarest flower up the mountain high, where the bravest had claimed to witness. An unlikely flower that fought the harshest conditions to bloom, to be seen, and then die.

I no longer had green pants.

CHAPTER 7

SMEARING A PIG HEAD FOR CHINESE NEW YEAR

Chinese New Year is the most celebrated holiday. As winter delivers the bone-crushing chill and skin-whipping winds, children and families get ready for the biggest festival of the year—Spring Festival. Traditional Chinese red opposing pairs with blessing messages come up on doorways; the occasional fire-crackers go off in the streets. Laughter from kids mixes with roasting meats, and the fragrance of grains makes mouths water. The raising of the red lanterns gives new hope for a happy, prosperous, and peaceful year.

New Year's Eve at my house was buzzing with activities. I had helped my mother sweep away the old year by cleaning the floor and dusting all the furniture. She had trimmed my braids and cut my sister's hair. Tradition dictates that for the first eight days of the New Year, one shall not cut hair. Hair, pronounced "fa," sounds the same as the Chinese word "prosperity." No one should cut "prosperity" during the New Year celebration.

A pot of stewed pork with eggs was always prepared in advance. Pigs represented "fat" or *fa*, prosperity. Mother also made fish, *yu*, which represented "surplus," and sticky rice cake, *nian-gao*, which meant "year high." I liked mother's sticky-rice cake because it had lots of nuts, fruits, and meats. A sweet dessert with salty meats mixed in was my favorite New Year's treat.

By evening, our family of four sat down at the table by the fire where baked sweet yams gave off a temping aroma. It was time to make dumplings together. With the risen dough, Dad was in charge of making dumpling wrappers. Mom and I put fillings in the wrappers and made dumplings. My younger sister dusted the trays with dry flour before and after we made dumplings so that the dumplings would not stick to each other or to the trays.

Mom's way of making dumplings was different from mine. Dad taught me the fast way, *Ji-Jiao-zi* or "pressed dumpling." First, put the filling in the middle; next, fold the dumpling wrapper closed; third, with both hands, using the thumb and index finger, squeeze the wrapper top closed while holding the dumpling's meaty middle in the palms. Each dumpling took barely three seconds to make. Mom's way was the traditional way. After filling the middle and folding over the wrapper, she pinched the folded flaps five times on either side to make a total of eleven ruffles on the dumpling. They looked like the ruffles on a Victorian dress. It was an art. It was also a test of patience and tenacity. It was a symbol to Mom—beauty comes from hard work.

At the end of dumpling making, my mother would also put a candy in one dumpling and a penny in another. On New Year's Day, when we would cook and eat the dumplings, the person catching the candy would have a sweet and happy year; the person catching the penny would have a wealthy and lucky year.

New Year's Eve was also the only day of the year when my sister and I were allowed to stay up until midnight. It is called *Shou-Ye*, or "Sitting up at night, waiting for the New Year." When the clock strikes midnight, fireworks and firecrackers are lit all over the country. The thundering and crackling break the darkness and light up the sky. It is said to scare away evil spirits and bring in brightness and grandeur.

By then my sister and I would be satisfied and very tired, and we would fall asleep almost instantly. I would dream about the mysterious good spirits the New Year brought and was always eager to wake up in the morning for all the fun to start.

I was woken up by the thundering drums and horns of the Dragon Dance.

"Brush your teeth!" Mom shouted as I dashed out the door.

I jumped and squeezed between onlookers and got a perfect spot right in front of the pavement, next to the dragon's head. There were seven dragon dancers plus a drummer and a piper. The dragonhead dancer was still in his teens, but the flair of his dance invoked nonstop accolades. Propped up on his pole, a golden dragon's head with red and black scales and green eyes moved up and down, side to side. The three pairs of dragon dancers in charge of the shoulders, the torso, and the tail of the dragon followed the dragon head's movements in unison.

From where I was standing, the massive beast busted through the air straight up and then twisted its body powerfully, as if to crush its prey. The gold, red, and black scales gathered wind and dust, and its emerald eyes stared menacingly into my soul.

I raised my hands to my ears to block out the thumping drums and realized that they vibrated inside my heart and pumped the blood to my head. I watched their routine carefully, fantasizing to join their steps at a moment's notice.

A pair of warm hands grabbed my shoulders and pulled me backward. "I want to watch, Dad; the lion dancers are coming next."

"Oh, maybe on the way, Morning Feather; we don't want to be late."

I remembered. The most exciting party of the year always happened on New Year's Day at Grandma's house. All her children and their families gathered and enjoyed the biggest feast of the year. I had been looking forward to seeing my cousins.

Dad laid four packages in a roll for us to carry. It contained half of the dumplings and cold dishes we made the day before for potluck today, carefully packaged china, drink ware, and gifts for relatives. The bus stop was a fifteen-minute walk away. With so much to carry, Dad would have to carry the load with his bike first while walking us to the bus stop. We then took the load onto the bus while Dad rode to the destination to meet us.

Bus 10 travels on the most prominent road, Chang-An-Jie (Forever Peaceful Boulevard), in Beijing and passes the famous Tiananmen Square. The middle of the road had been reserved for the New Year's parades. Troops of dancers and wagons with floats performed nonstop celebrations. In addition to dragons and lions, there were floats of pigs, roosters, horses, harvests, and lotus flowers. Dance troops wore beautiful, sparkly costumes. Drums and trumpets created waves of roars. My face was plastered against the bus window until Mom called us to help her unload. Dad was already waiting at the bus stop. We loaded up his bike again and followed the crowded path onto the side street to Grandma's house.

Even though it was not ten o'clock yet, all of the families were already gathered there. After all, my uncle's family lived in the same courtyard as my grandma and grandpa. My big (oldest) and little (youngest) aunts' families all brought bundles of packages with them. I was excited to see my three cousins. "Come on, Morning Feather, play poker. We've been waiting for you." We always started out with the simplest poker games, competing with each other. The winner collected chips and then used chips to redeem snacks. We were loud and obnoxious. Soon snacks and poker cards started to fly everywhere. That was when we got called by our big aunt to go wash up and help set tables.

In the great room, the adults' table had already been set. When the cousins and I walked in, we had to hush our laughter and ease our knee-jerk movements into halfway-decent manners.

The drop leaves of the big, round dining table had been raised. A white crochet tablecloth with roses peeked through the clear vinyl cover. In the middle, a huge blue soup tureen stood stoutly, showing off the double fish swishing, splashing in water with swaying lilies. Surrounding the soup tureen were eight English bone-china platters, all with blue flowers and vines. Four of them had steamed dumplings piled high, interspersed with four traditional Chinese dishes of stewed pork, pepper filet of beef, succulent roasted-duck slices, and steamed chicken. Smaller white dishes showed off cold appetizers and delicacies. For individual settings, each person had a blue-flowered Chinese bone-china bowl and a crystal goblet.

For the kids' table—wait, this table was not only for kids. Uncle's wife, our favorite auntie-in-law, always sat with us at the kids' table. She had proudly embraced her humble roots. She grew up in a factory worker's family that had so many kids that the parents told them to earn their own living as soon as they became teens. When Uncle was apprenticing to become a mechanic at a textile company, he fell in love with the girl who seemed to be able to do anything and everything without any forethought or humility thereafter. Embarrassment was simply not in her vocabulary.

Uncle was a smart man. He was always tinkering. He always wanted to make things better, easier, more profitable. At the textile company, after fabric, textile, or yarn was dyed in the color pot, unskilled workers, most of them teenage girls like my auntie-in-law, would have to manually get the textile out of the dye pot and transport it to the drying and finishing stations. So day in and day out, my auntie-in-law would dip her hands into seventy- to eighty-degree Fahrenheit hot dye, lift up the soaked thirty- to fifty-pound fabric rolls or piles of yarn, and put them into a wheelbarrow and wheel them to the next station. When Uncle and Auntie-in-law started dating, Uncle would come to the dyeing plant to wait for her to finish the last few piles of yarn. He loved watching her heaving and huffing to get the heavy loads in and out of the wheelbarrows, her apron completely kaleidoscopic and her fair skin stained by whatever color of dye she had been working with that day. In the meantime, her unstoppable mouth would shout out shameless jokes and the anecdotes of the day.

Uncle loved watching her and listening to her until one day, he decided to help her finish early so that they could catch a movie in the park. The minute he put his hands in the dye, he yelped, shouted, and screamed. The dye was so hot, he could not handle it. Then he tried lifting the heavily soaked textile roll into the cart.

He failed. He stared at the girl he had been fascinated with, now with a new admiration. Three months later, Uncle introduced conveyor belts and an automatic return dyeing process for the dyeing plant.

When Auntie-in-Law found out what Uncle did, she punched him in the face. Because of his new process, four out of the six dyeing-plant girls lost their jobs. Of course, Auntie stayed; that was part of Uncle's deal with management. Gradually Uncle automated the whole textile company, and he himself became a top-management team member. Auntie still worked at the dyeing plant, with a new title, quality inspector. Now all she and her partner had to do was to simply make sure the fabrics or yarn stayed flat on the conveyor belt to ensure an even dye.

Auntie-in-law helped us kids set the table the same way as the one in the great room: soup tureen in the middle, eight English platters, and white dishes all around. Then she distributed the matching Chinese blue bone-china bowls for everyone. "Why the fancy schmancy? What a waste of time. Now I cannot even eat heartily, for fear of breaking your precious bone china!" Auntie-in-law grumbled. I could see Grandma giving a disapproving look while Uncle suppressed a laugh. He loved Auntie-in-law. And the kids loved her. She always said what she thought.

But I also knew how important this feast was to Grandma. As the daughter of the captain of the Qing palace, she grew up in the Forbidden City and the Summer Palace, rubbing elbows with princes and princesses. Everything had a meaning, and everyone had a place. Over the years, with the Qinghai revolution, the Chinese revolution, and then the Cultural Revolution, she had lost almost everything and everyone. These English bone-china plates were among the rare items that survived the hardship. These beautiful antique platters, with the same blue flower-and-vine designs, were four sets of fours. One set was platinum plated on the rim, one set gold rimmed, one set silver rimmed, and one set completely plain. Each set was given to each daughter. Grandma kept one. Uncle received crystal goblets. Only during the Chinese New Year, all the plates and goblets came back to one place, the place where family came together. Everyone brought things to share; everyone contributed to the New Year's cheer.

⟨⟩

The second day of the New Year's celebration was always the most important in my house. Over the years, Mom and Dad had worked hard to achieve the status of the most hospitable and the best and most professional banquet. It had become a tradition that my aunts' and uncle's families all came to have a dinner party at my house to continue the celebration.

According to tradition, people abstained from killing animals on New Year's Day, so they ate food prepared on New Year's Eve. But the second day, in contrast, was really a meat festival, because killings resumed.

The tested-and-true fact of Mother's inability to kill even tiny fish had led up to the use of small butchers and vendors for fresh meats and fish on the second day of the New Year. The first to arrive were a pair of black chickens from the popcorn man and his crippled wife, neatly packaged in a foam box, with dry ice for cooling. From what I heard, the black-chicken market had been so prosperous that the two of them were thinking about expanding their little farm into bigger productions.

*[handwritten note: * popcorn man chapter]*

66

Then Mom and Dad came back with big baskets of fish, pork, beef, vegetables, and fruits from the farmer's market nearby. The whole family got into a frenzied buzz. My sister washed veggies and fruits while Dad and I chopped and sliced according to Mom's instructions. Mom was busy on the stove top. As we only had two stove tops plus one indoor charcoal heater, she needed to optimize the way she cooked.

The beautiful writing desk with burr-wood inlay worked as a prep station. Mom and Dad had painstakingly arranged to have a glass top with felt feet specially made for it to preserve its beauty. In the meantime, it would be proudly displayed and utilized. Our rustic wooden table was dressed up with lace and then covered with clear vinyl on top. Dishes of colors of the rainbow gradually filled the table. With the chicken and fish simmering on the stove top, sweet-smelling yams giving off a mouthwatering scent, Dad called us to take a break to have a light lunch together.

Reheated dumplings from the day before and stewed meats could hardly be called a light lunch. But I knew Dad only said that to contrast with the eighteen varieties of dishes that we were preparing for our guests to come.

⇒⊱ ⊰⇐

A sharp clunking sound broke out in the yard as Uncle Su kicked the big gate open, entering the courtyard. "Look what I got!" He swirled something big all around for the neighbors to see.

"Stop that; you will get the blood on our steps!" Xiao Liang stepped outside to protest.

"Ha, so what? I am showing off my big pig head for the New Year's feast. I earned it fair and square. What do you have to say about it?"

Da Liang, Granny Liang's oldest son, came out from behind Xiao Liang, who was still a teenager. "Su, take your thing, and go back to your house. We don't want trouble. But you know our religion. Please stay away from our doorstep."

"Your religion, you don't say. So you are afraid of a pig head, ha? Yeah, Muslims, you can't handle my pig!" As he said it, he took another step toward the south side. discrimination

Da Liang's eyes turned dark; he grabbed a shovel leaning on the wall and held it across his front. "Like I said, keep away from our property!" he hissed.

Su measured Da Liang's look and then gave a wave. "This ain't over!" And he stormed into his suite to the northeast.

I heard Dad sigh heavily. "This hoodlum Su is smart to stop here. I was worried."

We settled down again to eat, but only minutes passed before Xiao Liang screamed out," I am going to kill you, you bastard!" A big cleaver in hand, he rushed out the gate. "Xiao Liang!" Da Liang followed, holding the shovel tight.

"Oh Liao Tian Ye [old heavenly father]..." Dad slapped on his coat and hat, calling out to the neighbor to the west, "Brother Qin, come out and give me a hand. Lisha," he called my mother, "ask Grandma Su to come and get her son. Lives are at stake!" He ran with a voice that I had never heard before. Was that panic?

Soon most of my neighbors were outside the gate in the streets. Dad and Aunt Qin were holding onto Da Liang, whose eyes had turned bloodshot. Uncle Qin and Grandma Gu held Xiao Liang, who was cursing and struggling to break free; the cleaver in his hands shone icy cold glares. Grandma Su, in her tiny bound feet, was swaying beside her son Uncle Su. Su, spitting, continued his bullying words: "What, what? This is the street, public property. I did not do anything illegal. I am celebrating New Year's." Turning to his voice, I gasped; on the wall next to him, which was the back wall of the Liang family, written in still-dripping pig blood, were the words, "New Year Red!"

Now more neighbors gathered to watch, many people shaking their heads. An old lady from the neighborhood association came to ask my dad, rather loudly, "Teacher Wang, should I phone the police?" With that serious prompt, Uncle Su spit again and then mumbled in his mouth while following his mother inside.

"Thank you, Granny Liu; there is no need to call the police. We got this." Dad let go of Da Liang's arms but patted him on the shoulder, "Don't pay attention to jerks. I will have the wall cleaned up. OK? You need not worry. Go take care of Xiao Liang, your mother, and sister. You have responsibilities." Tears welled up in Da Liang's eyes. It was anger, shame, and the unthinkable ordeal. He called out to his younger brother in a shaken voice, "Xiao Liang, I think it's time we go home."

Father asked me to help wash the pig-blood characters that Uncle Su had smeared onto the Liang family's back wall, which was on the street for all to see. Father and Mother still had work to do to prepare for our guests' arrival and the feast. So I complied. The winter chills did not bother me; I worked up a sweat. The dust in the street and the dirt on the walls did not bother me. I paid no attention. In fact, I could not pay attention to anything, holding on for dear life, trying to push away the smell—the old, irking smell of pig blood.

⚊⧗⧗⚊

"It is a delicacy, you know." My husband pointed to the steaming-hot pot with floating oil flowers and shimmering burgundy-colored pig-blood tofu.

"I will try it with my chopsticks." My older son stood up and hunched over, trying to pick up the gooey, semisolid chunks.

For a minute, I could not believe what I was seeing. Then again, the smell, that heavy, irking smell of old, curdled pig blood reached my nostrils.

CHAPTER 8
TAI CHI TEACHER

Summers were good times. Summers were lazy times. When not reading, I often sat in a tree, watching people pass by. High up above any other's line of sight, I watched carefully people go about their daily life. There were stories and moments nobody paid attention to. On occasion, a dragonfly would land on a leaf, and I would stare for a while. Sometimes, without any sound or detectable movement, I would capture it by the wings.

Dragonflies are beautiful creatures; the colors of their bodies often set the tone for the colors of their wings. I loved the colors of their wings. The translucent, paper-thin yet strong wings showed off tones of the ever-changing colors of water and sky. And the darker-colored veins worked like leaded window frames, forming the structure, providing support. After admiring them for a while, I would set them free.

I knew Uncle Su captured dragonflies and cicadas by the dozens, and then he would roast them on open fires and eat them. I was always sad thinking about that. Yet, I wanted to see, up close, these beautiful creatures; I wanted to touch them and then let them go.

The time was 1979, roughly three years after the downing of the Gang of Four, who had controlled the power organs of the communist party and terrorized the nation with their ruthless oppression. For three years, the country had progressed in mixed ways. The summer of 1979 was an especially interesting one as Chairman Hua Gong-Feng and Deng Xiaoping argued over China's economic-development strategies. Winds in the neighborhood seemed to change directions. Dad still went to the Neighborhood Association every Wednesday to confess his sins toward the "Culture Revolutions." However, he was now much more willing and much more involved, maybe even empowered.

It was rare to see him frustrated after a committee meeting at the Neighborhood Association. As I helped Mom prepare the best meal of the week (yes, we kept a Wednesday feast tradition which used to offset the trauma of Dad's Neighborhood Association visits), I listened closely to Mom and Dad's discussions.

"It seems to be such a good proposal to relocate the Association to the courtyard next to the day-care center. I do not understand why Qu Bo, the colonel, has blocked it. What would he lose by such relocation?"

"Maybe you can visit him and ask him privately? I will make some more side dishes for you to take," Mom encouraged Dad. Dad did not waste any time. He went right after dinner, taking with him side dishes and the famous liqueur "Zhu-Ye-Qing" (Bamboo Leaf Clarity).

I was not exactly sure what transpired during the visit. We could hear Dad sing even before he opened the gate at the courtyard.

"Baoxiang, the neighbors are sleeping already; no more singing, please," Mom urged the red-faced, slightly buzzed Dad.

"No worries, I am done singing. We had a brotherly talk…After his projects are done, the colonel will allow the relocation. Oh, guess what—he is going to be Morning Feather's Tai Chi teacher."

"Wait, what?" I jumped off my bed and came to Mom and Dad's bed.

"Yes, the colonel explained that he needed to work on a project before allowing for the relocation…Needs some quiet time, no construction. He said he could teach Morning Feather in the meantime. Good Tai Chi teachers are hard to come by. Colonel is the real deal." With that, Dad folded himself into his side of the bed and fell asleep. But the news caused trouble for my sleep.

I had not thought about the colonel since the incident with the silkworms. Now that the memory had resurfaced, I still could not forgive him for Beadie's death. His arrogance and stubbornness made me angry and hurt. *Now what was the real meaning of him blocking Dad's relocation endeavor at the Neighborhood Association? What project was he talking about? Might it be, "Mark my words; I will teach you a lesson"? If so, what kind of a degenerate man was he? A colonel taking revenge on my father, who was trying to do good for the neighborhood, simply because I offended him?* The more I thought about it, the angrier I got, and the harder it was for me to sleep.

I had never told my parents about my quarrels with the colonel. I could not see a reason to tell them now.

I showed up at the colonel's courtyard the next Monday morning to start my training. I had decided that I would not yield to him, regardless of how difficult and mean he was.

"You are here to learn not to use force against force, but to yield to force and redirect," the colonel told me as I stood in his meticulously groomed courtyard. I wondered if he could hear my thoughts.

He took a mulberry tree branch and broke it in half. "This is you, young and brittle."

Then he took a long, smooth wood stick that was hanging under his window by a looped thread. "This is made from Chinese yew, also called ironwood, just like that bonsai tree." He nodded over to the tea table, where a petite bonsai tree rested beautifully on top. It was almost comical that the bonsai was less than ten inches high and very delicate looking. I could hardly imagine it could grow to a size where it could produce a stick of wood as long as forty inches, like the one the colonel was holding.

With the looped side under his foot, Colonel bent the stick and looped the other end of the thread onto the yew stick. "Ah, it is a bow," I cried out.

"Yes, this is where you need to be. Bend but not break, and then garner all the force within when needed. Release only at the precise moment." Like a flash, the colonel picked out three wooden arrows and shot them, three in a row, in the blink of an eye, all bull's-eyes into the three wooden logs placed neatly apart inside the garden bed.

I was awed.

"Now we start Tai Chi. First, and the most important thing, do a forty-five-minute Zhan Zhuang (horse stance). I will be back when you are done." With that, he left me and went inside his house.

From what I had read about martial arts, Zhan Zhuang, or the horse stance, is basic training. Holding the horse stance for long periods of time, past the point of fatigue, helps in developing root. Rooting is the ability to create a base for maximal efficiency in striking power and thus the ability to efficiently, instantaneously channel incoming force (whether a strike or a shove) through your body, directly (vertically) into the ground.

Now all the excitement I felt earlier dissipated. I had certainly learned the proper horse stance at PE classes. But forty-five minutes? I would die! No, I was not one for exaggerations. I estimated I would be exhausted by ten minutes. Then what would I do?

If exhaustion actually came at ten minutes, then ten minutes came really fast, and the rest of the thirty-five minutes were painfully slow. My thighs started to shake to the point that I had to heighten my stance.

"You are cheating," the colonel thundered out. He gripped my shoulder and dragged my shaky, tumbling legs under a low-hanging mulberry branch. "This is the perfect height for you—cannot stand up." Yep, when I performed a perfect horse stance, the tree branch was millimeters above my head, almost touching my hair. If I hated the colonel before, now the hatred was so deep that my bones cracked. And they did. My joints felt splitting burns, and my eyes seemed to burn with lava, too. I closed my eyes. I felt my body floating.

"Stand up." I felt hands on my shoulders, and I opened up my eyes. I had fallen to the ground. The colonel dragged me up from the ground and positioned me, perfectly horse stanced, under the mulberry branch again.

The colonel settled down to drink tea at the table with the bonsai tree. "The world has two kinds of energy," he began, "positive and negative, yang and yin, day and night. Neither can sustain forever; both seek balance through moments of stillness and change…"

Through acid tears, I watched the colonel's mouth move. Sounds reached my ears. His words stopped midway, replaced with sucking tea sounds and then words mingled back in. A piece of tea leaf stuck on his chin, dangling. Colors of the bonsai tree trunk popped on the table. It was a very small tree, but if I focused, it enlarged to the point that it became the forefront while pushing the colonel's oily, tanned, skinny figure to the background. He was very skinny. I bet I would grow to be taller and more muscular than he. Then, if we were to have a fight, I would win. I imaged breaking his tiny legs. I would step onto his chest. I would tell him that he killed Beadie, and now he would suffer the consequences.

"Stand up!" The cold grip of the colonel's hands made me realize that, for the second time, I had fallen to the ground.

This time, when I was positioned under the mulberry branch, I had lost the ability to think or do anything. I breathed necessary breaths, fearing that I would have forgotten how to do that, too. The colonel was still talking. I was still standing, not sure for how long...Then his face came rather close. I saw his eyes. I blinked. "Good job," the colonel said. "We move on to the next part. First posture, opening and then brushing the wild horse's manes..."

⚔ ⚔

"How was your first Tai Chi lesson?" Mom and Dad asked simultaneously. The floating and plopping onto the ground feelings came back to me. Would I tell them that? In the corner of my hazy memory, the arrows shot deep into the wooden blocks, three by three, all bull's-eyes.

"OK, I guess," I mumbled and went to change for school.

I told myself not to lose my balance and fall down as I knocked on the colonel's door for my second Tai Chi lesson. Knowing what to expect seemed to make things easier and harder at the same time. "If I can last forty-five minutes in horse stance, the colonel will teach me Tai Chi forms," I told myself.

Standing, knees bent, under the mulberry tree, my body seemed to scream all kinds of pain, much more severe than the day before. I tried to concentrate on what the colonel was talking about.

"Breathing is the most important. It will help you unblock your chi..." I wobbled again but did not fall. I resumed my horse stance, accidentally banging my head on the low-hanging mulberry branch.

"See, that's what I am talking about. Your chi is blocked. Keep breathing deeply."

I swallowed the tears welling up my eyes, suppressing the burning sensation on my bumped head by taking another deep breath. My knees started to tingle. I could not move my hands to touch my hurting knees, as I had to keep "the half-open palm at the sides" posture. So I thought about my knees and secretly moved them a little. It seemed to help. *Hmm, I will try again.* With every breath I took, I secretly moved my butt, my feet, my knees, and my hands in small, unnoticeable ways. I tensed them, let go, and twisted a bit, this way and that. Then I noticed I was looking straight at the colonel's nose, so close I could hear him breathe. I blinked.

"You are too smart for your own good." The colonel looked at me severely, but his tone was not angry. "OK, then, we move on to Tai Chi forms."

The colonel only taught me one or two forms a day; plus we reviewed the ones already learned. Open form, brush the wild horse's manes, the white crane exposing its wings, brush knee, and twist step.

"This is not a dance class," the colonel called out to me.

I knew, and I had been noticing the incredible air currents I felt surrounding the colonel's every move. Yet mine was simply a well-choreographed dance.

"Bend your knees. Think that your feet are the roots of a tree, two feet underground. Hands: carry thirty pounds when you move. Try again." I tried again, much slower, determined.

"Better. Have you heard of the slapping-water story before?"

"Yes, Shifu (teacher/master)." I wasn't sure why I called him by the proper name. *did not want to respect him*

"You may want to try it at home, and see if you feel the difference."

I acknowledged and left for home.

The slapping-water story talks about a young apprentice who sought the teaching of the Shaolin kung fu. But the Shaolin monks told him to slap a vat of water until it was empty and then refill it and repeat all over again. After a year, when the young apprentice went home for the holidays, his family asked what he had learned. Angrily, he replied, "Nothing!" and slapped his hand on the table. The foot-thick table broke into two pieces.

⊷⊶

I stood in front of my family's water tank, a nice ceramic vat, glazed smooth inside and out with rougher edging on the rim for easier handling. It took thirty buckets of water to fill. I helped Daddy do that often. The water faucet was by the gate, furthest away from our apartment. Dad and I often got rather breathless after we filled the tank.

If I slapped one vat of water and then refilled it each day, I probably would gain much strength and endurance after a short while. But for some reason, looking at my reflection in the water, the thought of slapping those precious droplets all over the place was not something I was equipped to do. So I changed into my school outfit and left home.

That day we had PE class, and the focus was on long jumps. The minute I landed in the soft yet supportive sand pit after a jump, I had a great idea. After school, I asked Min-Min to hang out with me and told her about my need to practice *jin* (force) and my idea of using the sand pit rather than slapping water.

We each built a sand hill on either side of the pit, as fast as we could, using the fewest pushes or pulls possible. Better yet, we had used only one hand at a time. We each built our first hill with eleven strokes. The soft sand might look easy to push and pull, but we were both sweating as we went.

The next task for us was to combine the two hills in the middle. This time it took much longer because we painfully realized that these tiny conglomerates of sand were rather hard to transport with our not-so-big arm and hand pulls. It took us more than sixty strokes to build the big sand hill in the middle of the pit. Both of us needed a break already. We lay down next to our monumental sand hill, and Min-Min was marveling at my Tai Chi lessons.

"I wish my parents would send me to learn Tai Chi."

"Seriously?" I looked at her skeptically.

"Yes, of course. I read about it. People say it is more than just martial arts. It is a way of life that builds the mind, body, and soul—and enlightenment even. At the basic level, you will build a strong physique and a calm yet agile mind. At more mature levels, you will start to look at people and the world differently, like a chess master looking at the chessboard and its pieces…"

I reported to the colonel that rather than slapping water and wasting precious resources and hard labor, I had resorted to pushing sand.

"What you lack in discipline, you seem to make up with creativity." I could not tell whether he was retorting or chuckling. "Let's see how you do today with Zhan Zhuang."

Reluctantly I went over to the mulberry tree and set up my stance. Before I could let my attention wander, a dangling house spider dropped into view, directly at eye level, not two feet away from me. It had a light-brown body, the size of the tip of my pinky, a lighter-colored stomach, and darker-colored legs. These legs worked in unison, and the spider went up the string into the tree leaves out of my view. I was disappointed, but it did not last long, as the little spider dropped back out into view again, this time connecting another silky thread into the previous one. He repeated his motions many times, and I could see a rather irregular web taking shape. In my mind, spiders built webs that looked like fishnets with a grand structure and clean horizontal lines connecting major vertical lines of sprays together. But I was surprised how this spider went back and forth between the two major lines. Soon I could see that, rather than a fishnet type of web, he was making a translucent weave, like a thinly spread cotton ball.

"Saved by a spider." The colonel walked over to me and watched the spider weaving with me. "Do you know how long you've maintained the horse stance?"

"Uh…" It occurred to me that I had not paid any attention to my Zhan Zhuang at all.

"Forty-five minutes, and you did not move a muscle—because you were completely focused on something else other than yourself. Most students will not be able to achieve this until three weeks have passed. I guess luck keeps finding you. Now come, let's do the forms."

With my continued sand pit plays, it did not take long for me to start feeling the wind at my palms when I performed the Tai Chi forms. My love of dancing helped me remember all the turns, postures, and routines easily. I came to understand that it was the colonel's intention to make the Tai Chi training difficult for me, because both he and my parents thought that I lacked patience and endurance. More importantly, they thought I was too proud and too stubborn yet quick to seek shortcuts when faced with difficulties. I was not sure whether the colonel had achieved what he wanted in my training. As much as he was stern and willful, he had to constantly adapt to my whimsical yet arguably acceptable ways.

The really exciting part of Tai Chi training would have been Tai Chi push hands. This is where you transform Tai Chi into practical use—to listen to force, to receive and yield to it, and then to redirect it.

As I got more fluent with my standard Tai Chi forms, the colonel started to add single-handed push hands to our training. We each took a front horse stance facing each other; with one hand behind our backs, we each used the other hand to push and pull. I failed miserably each time.

The colonel's hand felt like a cotton ball coming and going. I tried pushing his hand, but it seemed to disappear like a wave. And I tried grasping his hand (which was disallowed), but he slipped through like silk through a ring or water through a net. But then all of a sudden, I would find his hand on my arm or shoulder. The next thing I knew I was on the ground, not even knowing how I got there. I would get up, grumbling and stomping my feet, begging him to do it again. He would always tell me that this was the end of the training for the day.

"Be better tomorrow. This is where you use your dumb head." Nobody ever called me dumb before. This was infuriating.

For many weeks I did not feel any progress. For many weeks, I wanted to prove myself.

The colonel told me that I needed to stop trying to win. Instead, he said I needed to learn to listen and to yield.

I really tried, and really failed.

"If you are so smart, how can you expect different results by doing the same things all over again?" the colonel prompted me. "Try again!"

I took a deep breath and promised myself that I would really yield this time, rather than push back and be slung onto the ground. For a couple of rounds, I was able to control my urge to use any kind of force. Then I saw an opening. The colonel's hand was coming to me toward the left. I thought if I kept the direction where he was going, I could simply push him to the left.

With all good intentions, I started to direct his right hand to the left until I caught sight of a purple scar peeking out of his sleeves. Completely forgetting what I was supposed to do, I grabbed his arm where the scar was. "What's that?"

I was slung through midair, and my butt landed squarely on the table where his bonsai tree was. Although I narrowly avoided the tree, the ceramic pot broke into pieces.

The colonel rushed over and set me on firm ground. Looking at the broken pieces of the ceramic pot, he swung his arms around and gripped my shoulders. "You indolent child!" his eyes bulging with anger, "Look what you made me do! That's the only piece I have from her!" Realizing his emotional outbreak, he let me loose. "Get out of here," he panted.

⊨⊨ ⊨⊨

"Mom, is the colonel married?" I pretended to ask casually.

"Oh, why do you ask?" Mom looked at me carefully but continued in a frank voice, "Well, you know I always thought telling the truth would be best in most situations?"

"Yeah, I know. How to use the truth needs great care. Mom, I understand." I behaved like the young adult she always encouraged me to.

"Fine, then. Yes, he was married before. His home was in Huairou, a suburb about an hour from here. But when he retired from the military, I think he had a big fight with his wife and left her. He has been living in our neighborhood since then."

I pondered how to use that truth carefully when I came back for my Tai Chi lessons. The colonel behaved like nothing had happened. After we finished Zhan Zhuang and forms, he waved to me. "We are done for today. See you tomorrow."

"How about pushing hands?" I asked eagerly.

"We are not going to do pushing hands anymore. It is not fit for beginners."

"But please, Shifu, pushing hands is the real application of Tai Chi. You can't stop teaching it. I promise…"

He walked into his house without letting me finish. As I reluctantly left his courtyard, I noticed the Bonsai tree missing from the tea table.

When you are deprived of something, you crave it beyond control. As a substitute for push hands, the colonel asked me to do parkour, using the three wooden logs in the flower bed as a finish to each day's training. I had never given much thought to those wooden logs after seeing him using them as arrow targets on my first day.

The three logs seemed to be from the same tree, probably several hundred years old, thus rendering a very large meter-size diameter for them. Each log was about a half meter long, laid a meter's gap apart from each other. Lying in the flower bed and surrounded by morning glories and mums, they formed an earthy yet grandiose appearance.

My first task was to do consecutive jumps over each without ever falling into the flower bed. As the colonel did not require any specific movement for this parkour exercise, I found out that I could use several basic movements: jumping, vaulting, crawling, climbing, and swinging.

I progressed through some rather embarrassingly unnatural movements. Regrettably, I started with climbing and crawling first. The first log stood a meter way from the edge of the flower bed and just a tad shorter than me. I leaned forward, trying to grab on to it. I struggled with my hands and feet to climb up. Old dried-up tree bark dented my palms and knees. Bruises and scrapes started to appear; finally, I was able to half crouch on the first log. Looking around to see where the colonel was, I felt a pang of embarrassment. I was brought up ladylike, at least in the public eye. Sure, in my spare time, my favorite activity had been people watching while hiding high up in a tree, but no one had known about it, except for the colonel.

When I was raising my silkworms, I had harvested mulberry leaves from his tree, first from outside of his yard, and then I climbed up his roof. Despite his multiple warnings to stop, I defied him in the name of my silkworms—until one day, I fell from his roof into his yard. A favorite silkworm of mine, Beadie, died. I blamed the colonel for it—for not letting me harvest the leaves easily, for getting angry with me when I defied his prohibition to my trespassing. Now, crouching shakily on his garden log, I suddenly questioned who I was and what I would become.

I stood up on the log, shaking but determined. I realized how much I trusted my hands but not my feet. I had climbed thirty-foot-tall trees before without breaking a sweat, simply because I was holding on to the tree trunks with my hands. Now, standing up on the log, which was only three feet tall, I felt dizzy and scared, my hands uncomfortably hanging there, unsure of what to do.

I talked to myself. *It is only three feet high; you can land safely anywhere without needing any help. So why so scared? So what if you land in the flower bed? It is part of the training. The colonel cannot be upset with you. Or let him be. He's given me enough grief...Don't crawl. It is so undignified. Jump and swing; make elegant moves. You can do it.*

I did jump. My cautious calculations landed me short of the center, and I lost my momentum to keep going. So I stopped and balanced myself; then I made the next jump and continued all the way down to the other edge of the courtyard.

Things did get easier the second time around. Soon I was able to jump up the first log and then make three consecutive jumps all the way to landing.

The colonel then made things harder. First, I had to place candles on each log at my first run. Then, carrying a fourth candle, I needed to replace each one when I landed on a log. A further requirement was to make the obstacle run in under twenty seconds, so there was no time to waste.

With banged-up elbows and bumped knees, I was getting the hang of balance, control, and determination. On a day when I was just about to beat the timer, a rush of knocks on the door broke my concentration, and I stumbled down to the courtyard, almost landing in the flower bed. The colonel went to open the door.

"Colonel, I am your ex-wife, Pure's, son, Song. She is dying. She is asking for you."

I sat on the ground, panting, intrigued by the stranger.

The colonel did not say anything for a while. An uncomfortable silence seemed to last a long time. Then he responded, "I have business to tend to. Leave the address. I will go later today." Then the door closed.

I dusted up my pants and stood up.

"We do push hands." The colonel looked at me, emotionless.

For some reason, I became concerned for him. "Are you sure? I can come back tomorrow."

"No talking; let's push hands," the colonel ordered.

I set up my stance and followed his hand to pull and push. His face was blank without emotions; his hand came and went like clouds. But a feeling overwhelmed me; I searched his face, his motions. I felt the need to help him. And in an unconscious move-ment, I pushed him backward all the way into the garden bed.

He looked at me with a hint of sadness and an unmasked smile. "Morning Feather, you graduate today. Good-bye and good inten-tions." Then he turned around and went into his house.

CHAPTER 9
THE PUPPET SHOW

As latchkey kids, between 3:00 and 5:00 p.m., we roamed the streets, climbed trees, sat idly inside our own homes, or gathered with friends and played. We were elementary-school kids with two working parents.

On one of these boring afternoons, I walked past the new Neighborhood Association center. Instead of the quietness that was often there since my formidable Tai Chi teacher had allowed the neighborhood to build next to his home, a young guy, tall and thin, probably fourteen or fifteen years old, was playing with a puppet in a tuxedo and a tall hat. I curiously stared.

"Hey, how you doing?" he hollered.

"Good. What's that?" I wanted to touch the puppet. It looked funny, a little bit like Ronald Reagan, now that I think about it.

"A puppet. See, when I move my hands, the puppet kicks and dances." He showed me.

"Would you like to try it?" He handed me the puppet. "Reagan" kicked, bowed, and laughed. It was fun.

"Would you like to be in the puppet show?" he asked me. "I am Fu (Luck), by the way. I am the new activity coordinator here. What's your name?"

"Morning Feather. What puppet show?"

"*Three Little Pigs.* How about I make you my deputy coordinator first? We have some important tasks to do."

I was pleased with my immediate promotion. "What do I do?"

"We will need to recruit a cast. Come on; try on this puppet." He handed me a girl puppet with a bonnet. "We stand here and attract kids to come and sign up."

"What? That's backward. I have friends. Wait here."

I found Min-Min, Lele (Laughter), and Jin-Song.

Jin-Song was a very shy boy. That was probably why he was my friend—I got him to do stuff. His name meant Strong Pine; written backward, it was "Song-Jin" and sounded the same as elastic and was quite characteristic of him—not hard but adaptive. That was actually what we called him, Song-Jin. But the minute he heard that he was going to be the big bad wolf on stage, he turned purple. We three girls blocked the way, so he would not run home.

Brother Fu came to the rescue. "Don't be nervous. I will be the big bad wolf, and you will be the stage manager." Jin-Song's face gradually returned to normal.

So it was settled: Min-Min was piglet number one; I was number two; Lele was number three, and Brother Fu was the big bad wolf. Song-Jin helped running errands and provided feedback. It only took us a couple days to remember the words, but the preparation for a grand opening was much more involved. For starters, we needed to handwrite fifty plus flyers (we had not heard of copiers then) and build a stage—a puppet-show stage.

On the day that we scheduled to write flyers and invitations, Brother Fu came in late and told us his father was ill, and his family wanted him to take over his father's job at the cement factory.

"But you are still in middle school!" I exclaimed.

"I know, and I want to go to college." Brother Fu sighed. "But if I don't take the job, my younger sister will have to. Can you imagine her going into a dusty place like that and carrying cement bags?"

"You mean your dad cannot work anymore? He is still very young."

"There's something wrong with his lungs, could be cancer. The doctors recommended disability retirement. He makes forty renminbi now. If I take his job, I will be paid sixteen renminbi as an apprentice. And his pension is about eighteen renminbi. We are still six renminbi short."

"So did you talk to Granny Liu and ask for a stipend?" I asked. Granny Liu was the manager of the Neighborhood Association.

"Yes, but she does not have any budget to give me a stipend. Besides, if I take my dad's job, I won't be able to come here anymore." Fu sighed again.

"How about making boxes…" As I was saying it, I realized that making boxes would not work. The pay was very little. But I followed my train of thought. "No, no, no, not making boxes, making luggage tags for the train station. Our school does it as a way to make extra money for school supplies and to teach students working skills in the meantime." I beamed.

"You mean use us for free labor?" Lele said sarcastically.

"I did learn working skills!" I protested.

"Yes, you did." Min-Min nodded and then turned to the others. "She is really serious about making luggage tags."

Although her comments did not sound flattering to me, she was correct that I was really serious about making luggage tags. But the real reason was that I hated to lose, yet I kept losing to another girl—Coral. Whereas most kids could barely finish one pack, or fifty tags, in an hour, Coral consistently made two hundred tags, or four packs. I tried very hard, but I always had to use a few extra minutes to complete the four packs. At one point, I even sought Coral's advice: "Could you tell me if there is anything wrong with my process?" She watched for a few minutes, blowing her signature saliva bubbles and then said, "There's nothing wrong with your process. You are just slow." Well, *that* I could not accept!

I tried to find Coral's secret. I watched her carefully. She used exactly the same process as I did—spreading tabs across the table, brushing glue over all of them, folding them in half, and putting them on top of the luggage tags, dropping the tabbed tags in a box to dry while finishing all the rest laid across the table. Then she punched three holes in all the tabbed tags. Then she threaded metal wires through these holes for all the ready tags. Then she twisted the metal wires for fifty tags per pack. Exactly the same process I used. Only…faster.

I could not find her secret. If anything, she made it look so easy, so smooth. She toyed with saliva on the tip of her tongue while she made the tags. She almost did not look at what she was doing. Her mind seemed to be elsewhere.

Maybe I should be happy being second best, but it bothered me. However, once in a while, I'd surprise myself—when my mind was preoccupied with other things, I produced quite a few more than two hundred per hour. I think now I knew Coral's secret— she never cared.

There were so many things Coral never cared about, and she did not mind telling you, either. She never cared about team sports. She never cared about contests or events. She did not even care much about academics, at least not the kind that involved anyone else.

But she was good at most things, as an individual.

And that sometimes created trouble for me. As a student leader, I had hoped that I could count on Coral for support, or at least participation. But she was a lot more trouble than, say, your average student. She was not afraid to turn her back on anyone. She had a nickname, "her highness," and as soon as she turned her back, the term turned to "her heinie."

In the beginning, I used to "muscle" her into participating in the group jump-rope contest, citing a "one hundred percent class participation" requirement rule. She walked her heinie into the rotating rope, disrupted the whole procession, and made us lose.

After a while, I tried to keep her from destroying our team efforts. So when the spelling bee was happening, I chose a team without her. Yet the teacher said Coral should be in because of her academic rankings and disregarded my warnings. During the contest, she sat off to the side, blowing her saliva bubbles, and did not help the team one bit. After our class lost this event, the whole team was furious at Coral. But she simply turned her "heinie." I felt like I needed to say something, and it came out just as Coral blew out another bubble on her tongue. "Do you know what you are doing is disgusting? Not hygienic at all." It must have hit a nerve, because the next minute was not the careless Coral we knew. Her eyes narrowed, and her temple bulged, showing a mixture of burning anger and cold calculation. The team quietly gathered behind me. Noticing she was outnumbered, Coral shrugged and again showed us her heinie.

⚔ ⚔

I had to bring my mind back from Coral when Brother Fu seemed to get excited about the idea of luggage tags. He showed us how to make the invitations and posters. When Fu felt comfortable with our poster work, he left us to it. He himself walked to the train station to talk to the station manager.

The next day, we had huge piles of tag paper, glue powder, and metal wires in front of us. Brother Fu said, "Morning Feather, you've got to show me how to do two hundred in an hour. I can only do one hundred. Show it to all of us. I thought if we all can do a little a day, our activity center will be well supplied."

"My pleasure!" I picked up the basket. "I will first show you how to do one. Then, I will show you how to have your own assembly line to increase speed. But wait, you've got to make glue first."

So Brother Fu went to the room on the north side, which had a stove, to make glue from the powder he had gotten from the train station.

A few minutes passed, and I sent Song-Jin to see his progress.

After another grueling period of waiting time, I got anxious and went to the north room myself.

Pushing open the door, I stopped dead in my tracks. Brother Fu was licking the ladle covered with glue material, and Song-Jin had buried his whole face in the pan, shoveling the contents into his mouth. The room smelled delicious. Well, it was just your average smell of cooked flour dough. But these were the years when many families were still starving. I walked slowly to them and took the pan from Song-Jin's face. He eyes told me he was scared. I said quietly without looking at Brother Fu, "Be careful with this thing. Who knows what kind of chemicals they put in the flour to make it sticky?"

We walked back to the other room with the leftovers in the pan, and I proceeded to show them how to make luggage tags.

A complete luggage tag had three parts: a two-by-four-inch brown-paper body; a white paper reinforcer, about half an inch by one inch; and a ten-inch metal wire. The reinforcer would be folded and glued to the top of the tag, with three holes punched through to form a triangle. Then the two ends of the metal wire were threaded through the bottom holes and pulled out of the top one. This completed the tag.

In order to increase speed, I showed the team to brush glue onto all fifty reinforcers first and then glued them one by one to the tops of the fifty brown papers. Then we punched holes in all the reinforced tags. The first few were already dry when we started to punch holes in them, which made it a lot easier to punch and less likely to damage the product. At last, we threaded all the metal wires through the fifty punched tags.

Between the five of us, even at merely one pack (of fifty) per person per day, we soon had enough money to buy a few benches, curtain cloth, and a nice wooden box for puppet storage after a few weeks.

Brother Fu was happy, too. As he made enough tags during off hours, his father no longer pressed him to work in the factory. Things were going well for us. Best of all, our puppet show was ready. Invitations were sent, and both my parents said they would attend.

On the afternoon before the event, we were conducting our last rehearsal. The station manager rushed in and told Brother Fu he had an urgent phone call. Brother Fu went and came back, told us he would have to go to the hospital. His father was very ill, but he would try to be back for the evening show.

So we all went home for dinner and came back to the center at six thirty in the evening, a little before the show started. Brother Fu had not come back yet. The station manager became anxious and said we might have to cancel the show because there would be no one to play the part of the wolf.

I raised my hand. "I can play the wolf. I know all the words by heart."

"What about the piglet you are playing?" the station manager asked.

"I can play both. One puppet on each hand, and I can switch between the words for the two characters." I gave her a big nod. In order to persuade her, I put both puppets on my hands and read a part of the script. "Besides, people are starting to show up now. We cannot let them down. This is our first show."

She concurred but still gave me a concerned look as she exited stage right.

It was almost seven o'clock. I peeked behind the curtain. The theater was almost full. A few dozen people were sitting on the chairs and benches; another dozen were standing on the sides and in the back. I could see my parents chatting with a neighbor in the back.

As I was the deputy coordinator, I directed Song-Jin to turn the stage lights brighter. I walked onto the stage in front of the curtain. Immediately the room quieted.

"Good evening, everyone; welcome to our activity center. Today we bring you our theater debut: *Three Piglets and a Wolf,* played by Morning Feather, Min-Min, and Lele."

Echoing the clapping, the three of us started to sing, "Who's afraid of the big bad wolf, big bad wolf? Who's afraid of the big bad wolf? La la la la la." Our hand puppets danced and swayed.

Then the first piglet went to build the house with hay.

Then the second piglet, which was me, went to build the house with twigs and sticks.

And the third piglet went to build the house with bricks.

The first and second piglets finished quickly. We played around and laughed at the still-laboring third piglet. She sang the warning song to us. "If we don't have a strong house, the big bad wolf will get us." We just laughed and ignored her and went back to playing.

Now entered the wolf, which would be me again, using a very deep voice, singing, "I am a big bad wolf. I am out to get the piglets."

The first piglet saw the wolf and shrieked and ran back to her house. I, the Big Bad Wolf, followed. "I huff and I puff; I will blow your house in," I said with a low roar and rampaged through the house. The first piglet ran to the second piglet's stick house.

I, now a piglet, sang together with the first piglet in a high-pitched voice. "Who's afraid of the big bad wolf?" I danced with my right-hand puppet piglet.

Then I raised up my left hand to play the wolf, but I forgot to change my voice. So a high-pitched voice echoed about the whole room." I huff and I puff; I will blow your house in."

All of a sudden, there was thunderous laughter in the theater. I didn't understand why for a moment and was a little flustered but continued with the show. When my piglet number two started to sing again, when we ran to piglet number three, it dawned on me that I had been using the high-pitched voice for both the wolf and the piglet. My face was so flushed that my last victory song of the piglets winning over the wolf sounded rather sheepish, but thankfully, the other two girls were going strong.

We all came out with our puppets on our hands and thanked the audience. The audience clapped nonstop. When it was my turn to bow, I heard the clapping sound roaring loud. I felt so flushed that I did not even try to look for my parents.

When we got off the stage, I was surprised to see Brother Fu. He had just come in and heard all the accolades, and he thanked us for doing a great job. He said the most successful character of the show was the "Shrieking Wolf." That was what people were calling it now.

People gathered around in the theater room and the community room for hours afterward. More people signed up as members: a couple of retirees, a handful of school-age kids.

"Hello, Shrieking Wolf." Brother Fu came up next to me to help stack up the chairs. "I've got to thank you for the luggage-tag business. I have been getting very good at those and made some good money. When my dad gets better, he said he will do them with me at home, too."

"Good, I am happy your dad is getting better. Does this mean you don't have to work at the cement factory anymore?" I was excited that Brother Fu would be remaining at the activity center.

"Yes, about that. I am not going, but Ray—you know, the kid from the next block? He is going to take over my spot."

"What?" The shock left me speechless.

"Well, Ray's mother is getting disability retirement from the silk factory. She has glaucoma. Our two families are doing a trade. My younger sister will go apprenticing at the silk factory while Ray takes over for my dad at the cement factory."

"No! Ray is in my grade. And your sister is in middle school!" I uttered the words with shock as life's harshness sunk in.

"Really? Ray looks old enough. He might have fudged his age a bit, but people don't really care about that these days. Anyway, he's a good kid, doing favors for neighbors often. I guess he gets away with a few things. As for my sister, it's a sad thing, I know. But what can you do? She thinks it is an opportunity for her. Do you know how many people don't have jobs?" Brother Fu continued as if talking to himself.

I could not shake the impact of what Brother Fu had said. Ray was going to work in a cement factory? Was he even thirteen yet? We were going to graduate from elementary school soon. I had seen these cement-factory workers before—their faces and clothes full of dust, their backs hunched, their eyes gaunt, and their coughs… No, please, no. Not Ray.

CHAPTER 10

THE GREEN DANCE

China has been known to have some of the best ballet schools. The most prominent and oldest one was the Beijing Dance School, which was the cradle for the National Ballet Company. During the last few decades, Chinese dancers earned more than seventy major prizes (gold, silver, and bronze) in world-class ballet competitions, including the Varna International Ballet Competition, known as the Ballet Olympics, and the Moscow International Ballet Competition, known as the Ballet World Cup.

However, behind every success story, there were many tears and heartbreaks. Growing up was a journey to be savored, wherever we came from, wherever we were going. China, as a growing country, was also looking into alternatives, including, at that moment, green energy.

Long before entering primary school, I already knew that I wanted to be a ballerina. Mom said that both of us had strong legs and not-so-flexible backs. But our great stomach muscles would help compensate our shortcomings as long as we worked hard. I worked very hard—practicing day after day, taking every single opportunity in the community and at school to deliver my best performances.

On a gorgeous morning shortly before my elementary-school graduation, my school counselor, Shao, came to me with much excitement.

"Come, Morning Feather, we are going to the audition for the Beijing Dance School (now the Beijing Dance Academy)—three students from each school. I am taking you, Svea, and Min-Min."

I was Counselor Shao's favorite student. I had done everything she asked of me. I volunteered my time whenever she needed someone to fill in. I performed in so many shows and attended so many activities that I became a pillar of support for any school-organized events. Back then, it was very hard to find students to engage in extracurricular activities. There were no incentives for the students or families involved. People were struggling to make a better life for themselves. Extracurricular activities only consumed resources and time. But for me, my hard work was about to pay off.

Svea was not of Han heritage. She had large, greenish, sunken eyes; silky chestnut hair; and a very peculiar rear end. It pointed slightly upward and made her legs look exceptionally long.

Min-Min was often my partner in crime onstage. She enjoyed the spotlight as much as I did.

We arrived by bus at the Sun Temple Park where the audition was held. The gatekeeper directed us to spot thirty-one. It was on the far-east corner from the stage, which was still being set up. I looked around. There were several hundred students and teachers waiting in designated spots. Three men in green uniforms combed through different groups to select finalists.

After what seemed to be a lifetime, one of the men with gray hair came to our group. He pointed at Svea without any exchange with Counselor Shao.

"You here, bend down." He measured her legs.

"Raise your hands up. Close them above your head. Reach as high as you can." He let her stand there for quite some time.

"Do a split." She followed his command.

"Go wait behind the stage." He proceeded to move on to the next group. My jumping heart almost exploded.

"Wait," Counselor Shao called out. "What about her?" She pointed at me.

"She will never grow a ballerina figure. Too tall, no leg. Too much work on the back."

What did he say? I remembered every word because every word stabbed me like a knife, but I did not understand a thing.

"And her?" Shao became timid as she pointed to Min-Min.

The guy gave an impatient wave so obviously as to say, "Don't waste my time," and left.

The next hour and half was unbearable. Many groups exited the park. As Svea was up on stage with twenty other students, following music and doing dance steps, I had to stand there and suffer humiliation while waiting for her. I hated every sympathetic look as people passed me by. I wished that I had never come. I wished I could dig a hole in the ground and bury myself there.

Now that I think about it, I am sure I started digging with my feet.

When we finally arrived at the school door, Counselor Shao congratulated Svea, praised my graciousness, and continued to comfort Min-Min, who had been crying nonstop.

"Well, it's been a long day." She looked at her watch. In fact, there were still two hours left of school. She shook her head.

"Why don't you all go home now? Your teachers will help you make up schoolwork tomorrow."

I sat on the sofa that my father had made by hand and waited for my parents to come home. When they arrived, I told them the story. "Thank God," my father said. "You know what will happen if you get selected? You will be taken away from us to live at the ballet school. And if they think you are not good enough after a few years, they will dump you. By that time, your schoolwork is shot. They would have ruined you! Thank goodness they rejected you." Dad rubbed his hands excitedly. "I am hungry." He plopped down to eat.

Mom eyed Dad with disapproval.

"What? It's true. It is a blessing in disguise." Dad turned to me again. "You know your mother wanted to be an actress when she was sixteen. Even broke up with me because I disagreed. Took me months and dozens of poems and songs to get her back." Dad apparently enjoyed his accomplishment.

My mom, an actress? I was surprised, and for a moment, I forgot my own misery. In my mind, she was the most intelligent woman I knew. She was born for academia. *But acting?* Mom saw through me and nodded to confirm what Dad said.

Dad ate, talked, and laughed as usual. Mom and I ate dinner quietly. My sister winked at me and slipped away from the table without eating any vegetables.

I felt small.

I did not get up the next morning to do stretches.

I stopped performing at school events, or anywhere for that matter.

I read more and wrote more…

I started to win article competitions, some in the district, some citywide…

China's economic expansion was immensely felt by almost everyone. By the time I was in middle school in 1981, some people higher up had the foresight to organize a national article competition on alternative energy among middle-school and high-school students. Out of the thousands of students who participated, ten students won first prize—I was one of them. The prize was an all-expense-paid ten-day trip to the Daqing Oil Field in northern China.

I waved to my parents as the train started huffing north. I could not help my excitement seeing their proud faces fading away— my first independent days away from home. Better yet, I earned it myself.

I settled into the seat the camp counselor assigned me, which was across from a girl who was dreamily staring out the window. Something about her intrigued me. Her features were smooth and refined. Her hair, although short, hid just enough of her face to make you want to see more. She looked at you without looking in your eyes. Her mind seemed to be far away. It felt that she seemed to want to fade away from the scene. However, her body defied it. Even with my young age and my general ignorance of such things, I knew that she had the body of every girl's envy and every boy's longing.

"Hi, my name is Morning Feather. I am from Number Fifty Middle School in Beijing."

"Hi..."

"What's your name?"

"Julin (Bamboo Forest). I am a junior from Qiao-Dong High School." The school was also in Beijing, though it was not a very good school.

"What did you write about?" I asked.

"An essay."

"Ah, I mean content."

"I wrote about renewable energy around the world. I summarized which types of green energy can be used by specific geographical areas."

"For example?" I felt like I was squeezing toothpaste from an empty tube. But the topic was worth the effort, in my opinion.

"Uh, around the equator, solar power is plentiful; in South America, ethanol is readily available; in Mongolia, windmills...in Japan and Holland, water mills...and nuclear for some..." This was the first time I heard the term "renewable energy" with such ecological meanings attached to it. But the way she said it made me afraid that she was going to doze off midsentence. And there were so many midsentences.

"That's excellent work." I was impressed. She shook her head. I feared that she would turn away from our conversation. So I pressed on: "Isn't it wonderful that you found all the solutions with alternative energy sources?"

"No. It's useless. They cost more...and...they are hard to transport. For most countries with oil, it is much easier to drill holes... burn it up or...go nuclear." The sharpness in her tone made me uncomfortable. She seemed to be holding a grudge against the world. But strangely, I felt she liked my asking her questions.

"Hello there! I am Cece. You must be Julin and Morning Feather." This new arrival took our hands in turn to shake, and then she set down two bottles of water on the table.

"My seat is here, too. Counselor Van assigned us Beijing students to the same booth. I got water first before the washroom becomes too popular." She smiled her splendid smile and sat next to me. She was taller and stronger than me, confidence exuding naturally as she moved and talked. Within minutes, we acknowledged each other as kindred spirits. Cece and I talked almost nonstop for the eight-hour train ride. Both of us wanted to engage Julin. But Julin was rather standoffish at times. She alternated between minding us and fading into faraway land. It wasn't until Counselor Van asked her whether she missed ballet school that I suddenly started to understand.

A big red tour bus picked us up from the train station and took us to Daqing campus. *Such a big bus for eleven people*, I thought. We were so hungry that the walk from the dorm to the cafeteria seemed forever. Cece and I enjoyed and laughed over the infamous glass noodles with stewed pork while Julin deliberated over bread. Yes, they had yummy sweet bread, in addition to your typical steamed buns. Although not of great variety, food was certainly of huge quantities here.

When we came out of the cafeteria, dusk brought a gusty wind through the campus.

"Shalalalala…" The trees sang, and I felt they were calling me. I turned to the sound. I was awed by the most magnificent sunset looming over the forest.

The campus sat on the foot of the Big Xingan Mountains. The evening sun shone through the masculine branches of trees. It was not the orange color often seen in the city. It looked like blood, rich with iron, a deep-red color, with a hint of black. It was not flat but a sphere, breathing and withholding passion.

And the trees—what majestic things they were. Each of them not wide, unlike the old city trees, they went straight up and reached far into the sky. Their branches, intertwined as if raised hands holding each other, sang and waved in symphony.

"I want to go to the forest," I blurted out.

"I am cold. I am going back to the dorm," Julin said.

"I will stay with you, Morning Feather," Cece answered.

Cece and I chased each other into the forest. The earth underfoot was soft like a cradle and made me want to sink into it. I stopped, knelt down, and reached both my hands into the soil. The soil was moist, dark, and rich. My hands felt cool and warm at the same time. I thought I could just root there and grow.

"Look at the mushrooms." Cece pointed to the roots of a group of pine trees.

"Yes, they are edible." I remembered the ones Uncle used to bring to us from this land. "So are those." I pointed to the ones under the birch trees.

"Wow, that one's pretty." Cece dashed over to a red cap with white dots.

"Don't touch that one. That's poisonous."

She retreated.

"OK, let's pick the good ones and take them home," I suggested.

"You mean you will spread them out on the tiny desk at the dorm and wait for them to dry in the next ten days. And then pack them into your bag so you can eat them when you get home?" Cece grilled me.

I liked her keeping me on my toes.

"OK, we will leave them alone. Now what do we do?"

"We will look for different types of trees." That was very hard to do—for two city girls to apply what we learned and read from books into real life. Yet, we tried, and we recognized maple, hickory, aspen, and possibly a sycamore.

"I want to be a scientist. I love finding out how things work," Cece said.

"I want to be a scientist, too. I'd like to study something tangible, but not to look at a tree through a microscope and forget the forest, if you know what I mean," I said carefully.

"You will study people," Cece told me.

When we got back to the dorm, Julin, my roommate, was already asleep.

I was deep in dreamland when I heard shuffles and scuffles. I was a very light sleeper.

"What's up?" I grumbled.

"Sorry," Julin said. Then I heard the door open and close. The halls of the dorm, like many modern buildings at that time, had a very polished floor with poor noise insulation. Her footsteps slapping in the hallway were quite audible. Within seconds, I heard a couple of doors opening and people complaining.

Now I was wide awake. I wrapped the blanket around me and tiptoed out the door. Luckily, I did not have to travel far. Julin was coming back. I took her arm and pulled her inside. She was wearing ballet slippers.

"What time is it?" I asked.

"Five a.m."

"Ah, you would know." I yawned. "No, don't say sorry again. What's your plan?"

"Uh…"

"What were you trying to do getting up at five?"

"Stretch…I always do…"

"OK, stretch then." I sat back on my bed, the blanket still around me.

"And you?"

"Can't sleep anymore. I will watch you."

"I…I should not." She went back to her bed.

"Come on; do it." I jumped off my bed. "I will join you. Show me the ropes."

"Really?" She climbed down hesitantly. "Chairs, we need chairs," she said.

I put two chairs far apart, leaving enough room in between.

"You are not new at this," she said and started her barre position, going through the five positions of hands and feet.

I followed.

"Good form. Long legs. You should..." Julin started to comment on my workout, and then she must have realized something, because I could hear her swallowing very hard. I could not see her face. Whatever distant pain I was still feeling, hers weighed like mountains.

"Can you share with me?" I asked gently. "When did you leave ballet school?"

"At fifteen."

"How long were you there?"

"Five years." That was more than half of her school years.

"May I ask why you left?"

"Can't you tell? I got too fat."

"You are not fat. You are beautiful." This was the first time in my life I said that to anyone. I was brought up to ignore physical appearance. Mind over matter, I was taught. But Julin was truly beautiful, in a voluptuous way. God forbid that I learned *that* word in middle school.

"You are kind…thanks." She choked. An overwhelming urge came over me to comfort her. But I did not leave my chair.

"I was rejected by ballet school, you know." I thought some distractions might help her, so I shared my own pain.

"You are lucky then." That was not the response I was expecting, but maybe I should have.

"Yeah, someone else said that, too." I tried to laugh.

"Sorry, I didn't mean it…It's just…my world ended. Everything I worked for…sixteen-hour days, even weekends, five years and three months, all for nothing…"

"If you knew you would have to leave, would you have gone through it?" I was not sure whether I was formulating the question correctly, but I wanted to know.

"No."

"But why are you still stretching?"

"Because that's the only way I know to keep from ballooning further." The bitterness in her tone made me regret asking. But she went on. "I stopped in the beginning and gained twenty pounds in two months. And I had to repeat eighth grade in middle school. My parents hardly knew me. My classmates avoided me…Do you think I am weird?"

"No, you are smart and beautiful. Anyone who sees you would know that." I meant it and hoped that she would recognize it, too, so that she would stop hurting.

"Was there anything beneficial that you came away with?" I asked.

"Beneficial?" She laughed cynically. I felt the uncomfortable sharpness again. "Not that I know of. I was always hungry there. Nutrition was meticulously calculated and controlled. Or maybe they indeed starved me and made me think that they provided the best."

"You are a good writer." I kept trying.

"Well, we did read a lot. Ballet-related literature, mostly."

"Did you ever perform in the big theaters?"

"A couple of times. *Swan Lake, The Nutcracker,* and some other smaller pieces. But we saw many rehearsals. Even foreigners' performances…" Her voice trailed off.

"Were many students let go?" I had to ask.

"Yes, a few every year."

Julin ate a lot of bread that morning. I had to drag her out of the cafeteria. I felt responsible. But I also believed that talking was a good beginning.

The first day of tour was the drill sites. We saw many quarantined old drill sites on our way. Counselor Van said that they were still able to produce oil, but officials decided to close them up for natural reserves and for environmental reasons. We soon reached our first destination, production wells. A girl with plump features greeted us. Her rosy cheeks under the hard hat denoted much sun exposure. She was sixteen and had just started working here two months earlier. The oil wells built pressure to spit out oil every few hours. Her job was to open the valves periodically to let the oil shoot into the designated tanks in the ground. She said this was the easiest job on the field. No special skills required.

"Anyone want to try it?" She pointed at the wheel to open the valve.

Cece and I looked at each other and volunteered. We stood on either side of the wheel and tried to turn to the direction the girl directed. But nothing budged.

"Julin, help us," I implored. Even with all three of us, the wheel did not move an inch.

"Sorry I didn't mean to...Maybe the old wheel does not perform for strangers." The girl seemed to be more embarrassed than we were.

With her two hands held on to the wheel, she dug one foot into the ground (now I noticed her shoes had split in the toe areas), and her other foot kicked hard at the wheel pole. With a very reluctant creaking, the wheel started to move. She dug her feet one after another in a clockwise direction. After a slight hissing sound, her steps became easier, and a tar-like substance came out of the opening and shot thirty feet into the deposit. It kept spitting for another minute or two. She then proceeded to close the valve up.

"I then move to the next one. There are about twenty valves that I am in charge of today. After I get the last one open, it is pretty much time to come back to the first one again. Thank you for coming."

I saw Cece shaking her head.

"Don't worry. Brain people are not expected to be as physically competent," I said. She laughed.

Our next stop was the drill site. Those were the wells under drilling. A man in his forties received us at one of the wells.

"The drill head in this well was just exhausted. It is good for you to see how we change the drill head. *Xiao-An-ze!*" he shouted loudly. We heard clunking footsteps behind us.

"*Zhao-Si-Na-Ni?* (Are you seeking death?)" he said to the younger newcomer. We all turned around to look at him. This Xiao-An-ze guy wore a military hat backward. He swaggered past us. Talk about looking cool. Many years later, when I first came to the United States and saw college kids wearing baseball hats backward, I thought they were copycats.

"What? You know very well the brim of the hard hat would likely kill me quicker than wearing nothing. Why do you want me to pretend to wear it for these kids? Just so you can report that you didn't violate the hard-hat rule? Go do something useful for a change and get someone to make no-brimmed hard hats!"

"Not before I kill you first! Your mother will thank me." That was apparently softhearted harsh-word bantering.

The older guy turned around to face us. "I am too old; can't do this work anymore. This needs strength, smarts, and precision. Xiao-An-ze is nineteen and has done over a thousand drops..."

"That's right. You need a smart, powerful guy like me...What, you don't believe me? Hey, *ge-men* (brother), why don't you give it a try?" He challenged the one and only male student in our group—Awaru, a husky young man from Xin-Jiang (Uyghur) with long braided hair twirled on his head to follow the tradition of his nationality. He probably had been riding on horseback since he was born and hunted wolves and foxes regularly for food. Awaru slapped his hand on his right thigh at the challenge and charged forward. Both the older man and Counselor Van stopped him.

Xiao-An-ze cockily stretched his legs. He put on a pair of gloves with the fingers cut off. He pulled the metal chains from the pole down onto the ground, where the drill head lay, and locked it into position. Then he pulled the lever again to raise the drill head up. As the drill head moved, he gradually turned it closer to the pole. But the minute the drill head was completely airborne, it began to swing erratically. At five feet long and may be twelve to fifteen centimeters in diameter, it weighed a ton. The older man nervously spotted Xiao-An-ze, who used his hands and shoulders to moderate the wild swings of the drill head.

Now I could understand why the hard-hat brim would be unwelcome. It would have blocked some precious view. Even worse, it would be potentially deadly; judging from the closeness of Xiao-An-ze and the swinging drill head at times, the drill head would have bumped the brim frequently and knocked him out of the way.

But Xiao-An-ze got the drill head into a close range of shakes; then in one swift movement, he used one hand to pull the lever to lower the drill head, and his other hand and shoulder pushed the drill head into the chamber—I finally realized the pole was the chamber for the drill head to go in. Watching this completely marvelous yet brutal sequence, I wondered how badly Xiao-An-ze was bruised on his shoulders, waist, and legs.

There was a sharp screeching and hard clunking noise before the drill head completely disappeared from view. The chain now settled into a steady movement downward.

"There you go. Now she goes down two hundred meters." Xiao-An-ze took off his gloves and made a rather offensive gesture to Awaru. "I will see you at the party, ge-men!" Then he swaggered off, leaving us speechless.

The next few days, we visited many plants that used oil to produce household items, such as ammonia, soap, skin protectant, synthetic fiber, batteries, and artificial arms and legs. These visits were often a physical attack to the senses because of the fumes and smells these factories produced. Many of us got sick on our visits and often had to leave the group to get some fresh air. On the one hand, I realized how far reaching oil drilling was into our lives; on the other hand, after seeing these products in formation, I felt revulsion at the thought of using them ever again in my life.

My morning exercise routine continued with Julin. Sometimes we talked; other times we kept silent. At some point she started to call me "little one." It was not entirely fair to me; I might be younger, but I was a tad taller than she was.

The last day was a shopping day. The bus took us to the big city of Harbin, about one hundred miles from Daqing. The scene was quite similar to Beijing's own "Bai-Huo-Da-Lou" or "Hundred Goods Big Building (the Department Store)." A familiar phrase to describe the crowd would be "people mountain, people sea." I was very nonmaterialistic when I was growing up, until I experienced the "second hunger" in the United States. So after a few minutes, I went outside to wait. Counselor Van was there smoking. I remembered that I had never seen anyone smoking in Daqing—might be a regulation for the oil field. It was probably hard for a smoker like Counselor Van during this time. As much as I disliked smoking, I was happy to have company.

Van told me that people in Daqing and Harbin were quite well off because of the oil and its by-products. In addition, the Big Xingan Mountain area was full of natural resources. The forests produced a livelihood for people here, and the economic benefits reached far into other regions in China. Based on measured drilling, it was calculated that the oil here would last for more than two hundred years for China.

"Counselor, why did they use such a big bus for the eleven of us?" I was finally able to ask what had been bothering me.

"Gas is cheap here. Besides, they want you kids to have the best treatment possible. You are among the best, and the future is yours."

"So what is our next step? I mean, we all wrote about alternative energy, and you took us here, to the deposit and excavation plant for conventional energy. What plans do you have for us?"

My question must have pleased him because a smile crept up his eyebrows. He puffed a perfect circle of smoke and tilted his head to me.

"What do you think?"

This was one of these rare occasions when I did not have an answer prepared.

At the farewell party in the evening, the workers produced their best performances—a chorus not in concert, an off-key trumpet piece, and a poem read with heavy northern accent. Then they invited the student guests to perform.

I asked Julin to do a ballet piece. She immediately turned it down and became agitated. Perhaps to get revenge, she said I should be doing a ballet piece. I sighed and ended up singing a song.

But Cece danced to a famous Tibetan song: "The sun shines on Beijing's Gold Mountain; Chairman Mao is that golden sun…"

Then Awaru sang a folk song of Xinjiang that I had never heard before—about a young man's lover being married off to another tribe. It started mellow, went into anguish, and eventually came to a haunting battle. When it ended, people were quiet for a long time before bursting into thunderous applause. Even the young worker Xiao-An-ze, who had challenged Awaru a few days before, was clapping very hard. He was not wearing his hat.

Xiao-An-ze's short hair made him look more his age now. During the whole performance, he was casting looks in our direction. As soon as the disco music started, he came over to ask Julin for a dance. She refused. I would have accepted if I were Julin. It was just a dance. But Julin was Julin.

I was impressed by the strobe lights. Those were not the ones in the clubs in Beijing. The lights here were much smaller and cooler.

"LEDs?" I asked Cece.

"I believe so."

As Julin, Cece, and I danced together, I felt drunk with elation.

"Let's become best friends forever. We promise to meet together at least once a month, and we will work hard until all our dreams come true," I proclaimed loudly.

Julin rubbed my head gently with a tolerant smile and a hint of sadness that I had grown accustomed to. "Little one, you talk like you have the world at your fingertips. Dreams are useless...you will wake up...you will be old..."

Though not able to reach Julin after we came back to Beijing, Cece and I kept our commitment to each other for many years to come. We met every month at science museums, art museums, historical sites, bookstores...We went on to the top high schools in Beijing, and eventually we both went to Peking University and subsequently came to the United States.

But I thought of Julin often and always wished that one day we would meet again.

CHAPTER 11
A TRIP TO THE
EASTERN GORGE

Beijing Experimental High School was one of the best in the capital city—and in the nation, for that matter. The freshman class of two hundred came from all over Beijing after fierce competition in the Standard High School Entrance Exams. The school was as progressive as one could get. It was the first school that featured literature and political/social studies without following the standard syllabus. It had compressed, regular class sessions that ended at 2:00 p.m., and elective classes were offered after school.

For no particular reason, I started to use color coding for different groups of students—red for student leaders, blue for student athletes or jocks, and white for the academics.

The red students typically had a talent or two other than sports. They were the thought leaders, the movers and shakers. They made high-school life quite interesting, even if you were not part of that group. They often formed alliances among themselves. But it was rare not to see them at each other's throats, either.

The blue team was the most adhesive of all. They huddled. It probably helped because most of them stayed in *bu-xi-ban* (review classes) after school. Afterward, they had to complete a two-hour training or practice together.

The white team included the pure academics. They were not really a group at all. They seemed to care about academics only. They came and went individually and rarely paid attention to anyone or anything else. I found them to be ghostlike.

For my love of literature, music, and art, and my prior experience as a student leader, I imagined that I would naturally become a part of the red group. So I went to attend the recruitment fair, where different club leaders showcased their activities to attract new members.

The student-council president was a sophomore who came through the middle school on campus. The middle school here was also excellent, with a top ranking in the city. However, only one-third of the students were able to beat the competition to move up to the same high school. The student-council president had been an icon on campus, and I could see why. He was tall and handsome with luscious, dark, curly hair. More importantly, he carried an air of authority and a remarkable kindness in his ways. His name was even prominent, "Center Guard," just like the one in basketball, although he did not play any sports. I bet he would have been very good if he ever wanted to play sports. But no one would give up a more lucrative career in student politics. You could be paving the way for a bright future in college and beyond.

Center Guard introduced the Book Club first. He made it sound like it belonged to the white group. But judging by the committee members, it apparently went with the red group. He then proceeded to introduce the other seven clubs on campus: Newspaper, Music, Outings and Activities, Debate, Political Affairs, Intramural Games, and Athletics.

"Yeah, yeah, Center Guard, I see how you can pretend diversity through monopoly." An extraordinarily tall girl interrupted Center Guard and stood up like a tall pine among Japanese maples.

I weighed her words and checked the membership and committee listings. There were names that repeated often. All clubs were controlled by the red group except for Athletics.

"Hi, everyone, I am Amy." The tall girl continued to address us freshmen, who were clueless. "I am one member among my fellow athletes and our friends. Please allow me to say this—the athletic club truly has an open-door policy. You just show up and hang with us. You will be asked to help out at our varsity games. We need as much help as we can get. But do so at your own capability and willingness, all right. Showing up and cheering for us is good enough if you don't have anything else to offer."

"Yeah, Amy!" Someone started to cheer her, apparently from the athletic club. She waved to them.

"Oh, don't forget. We gather at the sand pit after school for practice and then for some fun. So join us there!" She sat down.

Center Guard gracefully smoothed over Amy's antagonizing speech and invited the chairperson of each club to present. The last person to come up on stage took me completely by surprise. Slender and meticulously dressed, she showed off her figure in the most flattering way. Her hair was long and thin but apparently treated to give it some volume to wave along the sides and on her back. Every nod of her head and every turn of her body seemed to call for a picture moment to capture the beauty of her smooth skin and the dynamic movements of her hair. The moment she spoke, I suddenly realized who she was. It was Coral, who had gone to the same elementary school with me. Apparently, she had spent her middle-school years right here, the best in the city. This was the girl whose academic achievement as well as her luggage-tag-making skills had made me jealous before. This was the girl whom I had insulted after her deliberate sabotage of an organized school event where I was the leader.

Coral was the chairperson for the school newspaper, the club that I hoped to join. I would not bet on Coral's forgetfulness or forgiveness. *Maybe I can try to smooth things over with her,* I thought to myself. Writing for the school newspaper would be a dream come true for me. It would be worth the effort to seek peace with Coral.

So I went to the annex building after school to look for Coral. The office for the newspaper was dark, and the door was ajar. I figured there was no one there, and I could leave a note for Coral.

It had been almost four years since the spelling-bee competition at my old elementary school. As the student leader for the event, I did not want to include Coral because of her arrogance and lack of helpfulness. But I had to yield to the teacher's recommendation to include her on our team. However, Coral was her usual self who did not give a care about the competition. We lost miserably. Out of frustration, I insulted her for being unhygienic because she had a habit of blowing saliva bubbles.

My behavior was unkind. It had weighed on me for all these years. If I had only criticized her on her uncooperative behavior, she would not have cared one bit. So I resorted to a personal

125

attack, which was mean and unacceptable. To make things worse, my friends at the event all supported me. If I ever knew bullying, I thought I had been the offender in this case. It was unbecoming for a lady, let alone a student leader who should have set a good example for others. I genuinely wished for a way to redeem my conscience. I thought I could write an apology and leave it in an envelope in Coral's office. So I pushed the half-closed door open.

Oh, goodness, Center Guard and Coral were tongue-locked in the chair. I immediately closed the door again, blushing and sweating.

As a general rule, dating was strictly prohibited in high school. Considering how progressive this school was, it should not have surprised me that some students would have been sneaking around together anyway. But being a "good girl" all my life, I had never seen anything like this. They were the top student leaders, and they had carelessly left the door open.

"Come in," Coral's voice echoed.

"Yes, please come in." Center Guard opened the door from the other side.

Neither of them showed any shyness regarding what I had just witnessed. For a moment, I questioned whether I was completely delusional.

"Morning Feather, right?" Center Guard asked. "I know you. You won the article competition. We could really use someone like you for the school newspaper. Have you come to pick up the registration form?'

Center Guard's fast-shooting words gave me no other option except for answering "Yes." I was still trying to digest the scene I had just witnessed.

Center Guard picked up a piece of paper and handed it to me. "Wonderful. Fill it out and come to tomorrow afternoon's commencement party to join, OK?"

"OK," I answered sheepishly, stealing a look at Coral, who sat quietly in her chair, watching me with an inscrutable gaze.

"Coral, it is great to see you again." I said to her sincerely, wishing for her to understand my apology telepathically.

"You too," she answered without any expression.

I folded the form, put it in my bag, and bid both of them goodbye. I wanted to get out of there as soon as possible.

As I rushed along the annex, trying to push away what I saw, a hand grabbed my shoulder. "Hey, Morning Feather, I have been looking for you." The chairperson of the Book Club stopped me. "Would you like to join our club?'

"Ah, thank you for asking. But no, thank you. I have too much going on already." I answered in an almost unconscious daze as I was still trying to get away.

The commencement party for the clubs was a big celebration on campus. There was music and food inside the grand hall, and oblong tables were set up for each club's registration area. Behind the registration tables, old and new members of clubs drank, ate, and partied.

I took out my neatly filled-out form and searched for the Newspaper table, where I found Coral behind a white, cloth-covered table with gold and silver tassels adorning the front.

I walked toward her and was delighted that she saw me, too, and walked around the table to greet me. This was the reception that I had hoped for. I reached out my hand to turn in my registration form. But before I could speak, I heard Coral's voice coming through a loudspeaker and realized that she was wearing a microphone on her shirt.

"Hi, Morning Feather, you didn't have to come, you know." Coral's voice was loud and clear.

"Wait, what?" I did not understand.

"Yes, I just heard from the Book Club that you have decided not to join *any* clubs after all. You mentioned how busy you are and how much you wanted to concentrate on your studies, among other things," Coral said matter of factly, with a cold, calculating smile on her face.

I was so dumbfounded that I searched her face for a second and then looked around. Center Guard was looking at us with apparent disbelief. Everyone else was simply taking in what Coral was saying.

"Yes, I will take care of this useless registration form for you." Coral ripped the form away from my frozen grip and tore it apart with a loud screeching sound coming through the loudspeaker.

All of a sudden, I understood. Coral had managed to shun me from all the clubs. She *did not* want me to join *her* newspaper club—or any club. Center Guard's apparent interests in my writing skills probably did not help the matter. Now Coral's open announcement, a lie that only I knew, was a perfect scheme to prevent me from ever joining the Red regime.

And there was nothing I could do.

I would have to call it karma. Payback is a bitch; I remembered the saying. For years, I regretted my unkind remarks toward Coral after the spelling bee. When I saw her again here in high school, I had hoped to ask for her forgiveness so that we could potentially work together at the newspaper. Now that hope, like that piece of paper, which held my meticulously filled-out credentials, was torn apart.

"Yeah, why not?" I kept my composure and returned Coral's stare with a smile, equally cold. Then I shrugged my shoulders, turned around, and walked out.

It might as well be this way, I thought to myself. *This was one way to end things.* As I left the flashily decorated conference hall, I felt pale in my own appearance. I passed the athletes and peripherals by the sand pit, about thirty of them shoveling each other, playing physical games. I felt a pang of loneliness. I had such an urge to walk over to them, to sit down along the sand pit and pretend I belonged. But I could not stop just yet. I needed to keep walking and let my disappointment, guilt, and embarrassment pass with each of my steps.

⟞⟝ ⟞⟝

In an effort not to turn ghostly like the whites, I started to come into the peripherals of the jocks. The jocks did not mind me being there, even though I had no sport to participate in. They seemed a happy bunch. Typically, during after-school hours, when many of us were doing elective classes, the jocks had to stay in *bu-xi-ban* (review class). Many of them needed extra help with academics. At about 3:30 p.m., they would start their varsity practices for two hours. Afterward, sweaty and gummy, they rushed to the dining hall with all of us, disgustingly smelly and disgustingly happy.

From 7:00 to 9:00 p.m., it was study time for all boarders. Quietness was required in the classrooms. However, when 8:45 p.m. approached, snickering and laughter often broke out in my classroom, where the jocks gathered in the back.

Red Heart often started to walk back toward his gang around this time. His specialty was long-distance running. Unlike most of the jocks (girls included), he was not extraordinarily tall. That did not really justify him sitting in the front row. Supposedly he told the teachers his eyesight was rather poor, which, according to the jocks, was merely a ruse. They said the real reason was that he liked to get into the dining hall early, and he liked the spaciousness in the front of the classroom, his legroom.

Every day when he passed me to join his gang for a chuckle before bedtime, I would start to clean up my desk area and prepare for the next day. But today I was rampaging through my bag and my pencil case, looking for my compass.

"You dropped this." Red Heart picked up my compass and put it in front of me.

"Thank you. Oh, I was silly, looking all over for it." I breathed a sigh of relief.

"Now that you've found it, would you like to join us in the back?" Red Heart made an unexpected invitation.

"Sure…of course." I would never refuse any polite invitations. But my heart was jumping a bit as I followed Red Heart to the back of the room.

The jocks, they must think I am an alien, which they are, to me, I thought.

Amy stood up to greet me. She was the tallest girl in school and the varsity captain.

"Morning Feather, your presence honors us," she joked.

"Oh gosh, Amy, I am the one who's honored. I have no talent in sports and don't deserve to sit among you," I replied.

"Well, you better stop that nonsense. Can you honestly say you academics don't look down upon us? You think we are not smart enough and that sports are all we have." Amy was not shy about being blunt.

"Not me. We are all talented in our own ways. We all deserve to be treated equally." I forced myself to utter these words.

I felt myself blush, because Amy did reveal my internal truth. My arrogance against the jocks, although never explicit, nonetheless existed. Red Heart looked up at me as if seeing through my lies. I managed a smile toward him. My words, although did not reflect truth before, I had vowed then to abide by them going forward. Because inside my heart, I knew it would be the right thing to do.

"You are wrong again." Amy patted me on the shoulder. "We jocks think *we* are the best. We are not as evasive and pretentious as you all. We know what we are good at, and we are proud of it. We compete with each other in an open, clean, and fun way."

"I am impressed by what you said." I looked at Amy genuinely. "You are right; you guys are the most open, honest…and fun! I truly hope I can become part of you guys."

"Yeah, good; then you better show us how to do this question for tomorrow's test first."

"Oh, an ulterior motive, Amy? I thought you all don't manipulate people." I happily helped. I felt useful for the first time in high school. I felt I belonged for the first time in high school.

I started to look forward to the end of self-study each evening. When Red Heart walked by me, I was more than ready. Me and the jocks, we talked—about news, movies, books, dumb questions teachers gave us. On occasion, I left the talking to them. They liked to joke about other students. Even though I refrained from talking about others, I knew that the jocks were honest about their opinions. To them, there was a big wide world out there, full of adventure and fun, where studies and status meant very little. I tried to make myself useful to them. I helped with homework questions, managed supplies, and ran errands at varsity meets. Both Amy and Red Heart became my friends.

Varsity regional competitions would start right after National Day, which was October 1. The team often had a group outing together in advance of the competitions, basically a last hurrah before stringent competition schedules and practices. I was very happy that Amy invited me to join their overnight outing to the Eastern Gorge on Saturday, just before the national holiday. As Friday rolled around, and I was packing up for home, Amy rushed over to me and said, "Morning Feather, there is inclement weather tomorrow; give me your phone number, and Red Heart or I will call you if we change plans about the outing."

I prayed the whole time for good weather. Saturday was cloudy and gray, but no phone call came. So I packed up a messenger bag full of food and snacks and set out to meet the varsity team at Jian-Gou-Men Outside Station at 4:00 p.m. As I walked up to the platform of the station, where the number 997 long-distance bus would take travelers to the Eastern Gorge, I knew something was not right. There were only a few passengers waiting for the last bus. It certainly did not look like the varsity team would have any presence there. My heart sank. I knew now. They had changed plans, and they forgot to tell me.

"Morning Feather." A voice roused me from my sad preponderance.

"Red Heart, I am so happy you are here. I thought the plans changed. I thought varsity canceled the outing. Where's…" My heart became happy again, and I started to look around.

"I am sorry, Morning Feather. The plan did change, and Amy asked me to call you, and I didn't." Red Heart looked at me anxiously.

"But I came all this way…" Tears were about to come up, and I quickly suppressed them. No way was I going to cry in front of anybody, let alone a boy.

"That's just the thing." Red Heart searched my eyes. "I still want to go." He paused, "And I want to go with you. Even if it is just the two of us. If you are willing, of course," he said slowly.

Now it was my turn to search his eyes. This unexpected turn of events stumped me. But I would never admit being stumped, ever.

I had never noticed his eyes before. They were big and gray. The whites and the iris seemed to melt into each other, like a vast pool of water, a brush painting. His pupils were rather large and dark. Little speckles of light shone around them, pulling you toward the center, the dark, mysterious well of the unknown. There was something simmering and something yet to be discovered hiding far below the surface...

"Err...what are you thinking?" Red Heart stuttered, and he blinked away the dark waters.

"Yes, I will go." Surprised by my firm answer, Red Heart looked up with his eyes foggy and sparkly at the same time. I wanted to grab the fires in his eyes, but he quickly avoided my stare.

It took almost an hour and half of long-distance bus riding to arrive at the entrance of the Eastern Gorge. As soon as we got off the bus, we knew that our plans were in shambles.

The resort lodge was dark and locked. Apparently, it had closed due to inclement weather, and there were no tourists—or anybody, for that matter—around.

"There goes our plan to rest for the night and explore in the morning," Red Heart said dejectedly.

"Hmm, mind you that we also missed the last bus back to town. So we are stuck here. Either we move forward, or we move forward." Since there was little choice as to what we could do, I was actually excited about starting the tour. The autumn day was just turning into dusk. There was a mist rising up from the mountains along the gorge. The mystery and adventure awaited.

"You don't act like a girl." There was some surprise in Red Heart's voice.

"Err, thanks! Should I take that as a compliment?" I flashed a look at him and started onto the path to the gorge.

"Yes, you should," Red Heart said and smiled. "Nothing seems to faze you. And…" now he was panting behind me, "you don't show any weakness or distress like the well-pampered and perfectly sheltered girl you portrayed."

I was very pleased to hear his praise and thankful that he could not read my proud facial expression from the back.

The winding path was still visible under the evening sky. "One hundred li round-trip (thirty miles); if we walk ten li an hour, it will take us ten hours to go to the top and then back. But I guess we are walking faster than that, probably close to twenty li an hour now," I declared casually to Red Heart, who was walking beside me as the path widened where a stream of river appeared next to us.

"You are good at math; I get it. I just never figured you are any good at…this—walking or any physical exertion kind of thing." Red Heart praised me again while quieting his footsteps, his breathing undisturbed, deep and even. I could see his long-distance running training paying off. I also could not help thinking of the colonel, my Tai Chi teacher, realizing his gift to me at this unexpected moment.

"My dad became an engineer finally," Red Heart told me all of a sudden.

"That's great. What does he do?"

"He builds dams and bridges."

I laughed.

"What's to laugh about?" Red Heart asked, puzzled.

"Dams to separate things; bridges to connect things. I laugh at the irony," I explained. "But congratulations to him. Was that difficult to achieve?"

"Difficult for him. It has been eight years. You know, his generation did not have formalized higher education. A college degree is required for engineers now. For the last eight years, he had been taking adult continuing education classes in the evening, and he got his college degree equivalent in the summer."

"Yes, I understand. My parents have been teaching adult education. The students are very admirable, they say."

"My family is very proud of him. I will be the first one to have a real college education, you know." He happily touched my arm.

"But I thought you have an older brother. Isn't he going to college first?" I asked inquisitively.

"Hmm…" Red Heart seemed to grumble in displeasure. "He is not going. He has a business now. He is the golden boy of the household. He can do no wrong."

"OK, first-generation college boy, you better work harder on your academics, then." I jokingly pushed him in an effort to divert the tension I sensed between him and his brother.

"Well, aren't you the little bragger!" he said and pushed back, and I lost my footing.

"Ouch," I exclaimed as I fell into the little stream next to me.

"Oh my, I am sorry!" Red Heart reached out and dragged me up onto the bank.

"Oh, no problem, no damage done." I shrugged and kept walking.

The stream was about one foot deep, and it was just deep enough to get my shoes wet. As I walked in my wet shoes, I started to worry. These were my only pair of sneakers. They were made of burgundy suede with a nice, cushioned footbed. I could feel the water swish and swash with each of my step. *Am I going to ruin these shoes?* I thought to myself.

"Unlike you, I am not counting on going to a top college somewhere. I want to become an engineer too. There are many technology colleges in the city. They will do just fine," Red Heart said lightheartedly. "I like tangible things, things I can touch and feel. Maybe I will design a bridge and build it, or design a car, totally aerodynamic and energy efficient. What do you want to do?"

"I want to...design a new human race...free from all the troubles and flaws of the world. This new species will only do what's right, and they will always know what's right."

"You are outrageous. What do you have against the real people? Didn't the troubles of the world make us who we are? Our own struggles of right and wrong wrote histories of evolution and human progression. Isn't every flaw, deeply embedded, a way to perfection and vice versa?"

His tone of angst and righteousness pulled me back from my exaggerated claims.

"You can't tell I am joking, can you?" I asked sheepishly.

He turned around to look at me. "Actually, no. You have been full of surprises, truth be told. I don't know what to expect." Red Heart shook his head and walked on. I followed him around a bend into a big clearing. Both of us came to a stop.

The first thing we saw was the moon, big, bright, and beautiful, almost round, shimmering in a perfectly preserved basin of water. As our eyes traced upward, hanging heavily and serenely, she looked back at us, with gracious reach and heavenly embrace. Neither of us said a word. It was too beautiful to make a sound.

Stealthily, I looked around. The round lake was surrounded by the looming edges of the mountains. Mist still rose in the night, separating our world and everything else. It was a fairy tale, a dreamworld, where we were. Only in this world, your wishes could come true.

Red Heart built a fire and carefully put rocks and stones around it. "Although unlikely, I want to make sure that we don't cause a forest fire," he explained to me.

I nodded.

"It is almost midnight. Maybe you want to get some sleep?" he asked.

"No, I don't think I can sleep." I moved my feet uncomfortably in my shoes, and he noticed.

"Let me see." He reached for my feet.

"No need." I tried to push him away.

"Stop being silly." He looked at me severely and took off one of my shoes.

"Gosh, your shoes are completely wet. How could you not tell me? This whole time you were walking like this?" He proceeded to take off my sock.

"Stop! I am fine!" I protested, one foot in his hands.

"You stop, and you are not fine. I don't see any blisters. That's good. Now let me dry your socks."

Now I was looking at my bare feet, and tentatively, I looked at him. Red Heart worked hard to wring my socks dry and squeezed my shoes until no water was leaking out. And then he took the warm stones and put one in each of my shoes and inside my socks.

He left them next to the fire. He turned around to look at me, and I looked at my bare feet.

"Come here." He took my feet and wrapped them in his scarf.

"No, you don't want my feet smelling around your neck." I protested again.

"No, but it is better than you get sick. Illness comes from cold feet. Don't you know?" He criticized me, like a parent disciplining a child. I did not know whether to feel embarrassed or to be thankful. It had been a while since anybody had talked to me like this. Ever since I turned a teen, even my parents were always polite with me.

Trying to change the subject, and also in an effort to make up for the earlier conversation of my unintended offense to "real people" of the world, I told him that I wanted to become a child psychologist, helping kids with all kinds of difficulties facing the world. He seemed to approve. I did not know when it started to matter to me whether he approved or not.

He came over to check on my feet, and he gasped." They are ice-cold!"

"They will get better." I tried to ease his concern.

"Not unless I try something else." He unwrapped the scarf as he mumbled.

He turned to face me and looked sharply into my eyes. "I am trying to help you, so go with it." Before I could even understand, he lifted up his shirt, took both of my feet, and put them inside, right on his chest.

"No!" My natural instinct took over, and I started to push him away. With my feet up high on his chest, my body scrunched up uncomfortably, my flailing arms and hands hit his shoulders and head.

"Stop it!" With the left hand holding my feet in place, his right hand grabbed my left shoulder and pushed me down on to the ground.

I could not even begin to describe the shock. He was right on top of me, his breath inches away. I could feel the force of his hand on my shoulder. Tears welled up in my eyes. My feet, squarely on his chest, were separating us, but most of his body weight was on them, pressing down on me.

Time seemed to stand still. Neither of us moved.

I noticed his breath was short and ragged, and I felt the rapid thumping coming from my feet. His heart, on the brink of bursting open, was beating an unsustainable quiver.

I managed to look over into his eyes; those grayish ponds of mysterious waters from before had now turned into melting lava with droves of heat waves raging over. He once again turned away his eyes. I detected guilt and pleasure seething through his avoiding lens.

"I am going to sit back now. Please don't make this more embarrassing for both of us." His voice was almost pleading.

Red Heart sat back down slowly, with my feet on his chest. He turned slightly to face the fire. The twinkling bluish-red flames now had become a crackling orange fair, dancing admirably in the crisp night air.

Red Heart's beating heart had changed into a sturdy, rhythmic drum, vibrating not so subtly through my toes and legs. A gradual wave of warmth also invaded me from my feet up, and it was felt in my stomach. I turned my head to look to the looming edges of the mountains and the moon, now smaller but brighter. She carefully watched back, as if she could see through me, but in an understanding way, no alarm, no disapproval, just acceptance. I felt calm in her presence, in her embrace.

Then a thin veil hid her face. A light breeze came over. I noticed the fire was at its last dance.

Red Heart let go of my feet and said, "They are warm now. Your socks are dry, too." He put them on for me. "Do you want to sleep while I gather some more wood for the fire?"

"No, I can't sleep; let me help."

The fire was crackling again. I was amazed at the way he constructed it, almost like a tepee. He showed me. "The key is to stabilize these supporting sticks. I used crisscross patterns at the base. Two birds, one stone. You have a nicely burning base while securing the top structure. This way air can come in to feed the flames."

"Air and fire are companions while water and fire are enemies." I looked over toward the pond.

"Now that we are onto elements, let's see. Air and wood are enemies; wood and fire are companions; we don't have metal here. Metal and wood are enemies…" We lost count. So I sighed and said, "Everything is meant to work together." I helped build the fire higher.

We were so focused that the sizzling raindrops on our fire took us by surprise.

"It's raining," Red Heart said, alarmed. "We need to find shelter."

"Can't we just walk in the rain?" I was feeling confident by the experience so far.

"Not for long. If we are not careful, we could get hypothermia. We are at the peak of the valley. Just the halfway mark. Let me go over that hill to see if there is anywhere we can hide. Wait here."

Red Heart broke into a run; the night outlined his figure on top of the mountain, and then he quickly disappeared from view.

I was almost shocked when I noticed that the big, beautiful fire we had built together vanished in a few heavy poundings from the rain. Then I felt it—the heavy hitting on my head and body, the most excruciating beating I could ever imagine. I looked up, scared, and felt the heavy, sharp rain knifing at my face. I buried my face in my hands and started to cry. "Red Heart, where are you?"

"Red Heart, where are you?"

"Where are you?"

"Where are you?"

The mountain echoed. My voice bounced around, from strong to limp, just like my body being thrown back and forth until the life force within started to give in.

I scrunched up trying to run toward where I had last seen Red Heart's figure. The heavy knives chased me, cut into me, and tortured me. "Red Heart!" I cried out in desperation.

"Yes, I am here!" Red Heart descended from the peak. I struggled uphill toward him.

"Are you OK?" He reached out his hands, alarmed by the panic in my voice.

I had been walking five hours before we came to the lake. Since we sat down, I did not have any food or sleep. I was exhausted, hungry, and cold, and the rain just took away any remaining strength I had. And the harshness of it all made me feel that I was going to die. I needed help. Red Heart was right there, his arms open, ready to embrace me. And I *really* needed him. I wanted to run into those arms, put my head on his chest. I wanted to hear those heartbeats again, those warm, strong sounds of life. I wanted him to hold me, to keep me safe and warm, to tell me everything was going to be OK.

I hated myself for it, for feeling this way. I hated him for making me feel that I needed him.

I steadied myself, resisting the urge to lean on Red Heart. "I think so. I just got a little dizzy." With a deep breath, I understood that I could fake it until I made it.

"I found a cave right below the peak. Come, it will give us shelter." I followed Red Heart's footsteps, trying not to stumble.

A fire lit up the stone cave with unimaginable warm and comfort. I was still wet from the rain, but what a difference it made! A shelter, maybe eight feet in height, width and depth, was big enough for building the fire and comfortable enough for us to settle ourselves and our supplies. I noticed that there were pine needles on the ground and guessed that there must be a pine tree towering above the cave, standing tall in all kinds of weather, unyielding, shedding needles but never a tear.

Red Heart poked a stick at the crackling fire. I made peanut butter and jelly sandwiches for both of us.

Warm air and food set my mind adrift…

I looked at the pine needles next to my feet, and I looked up at the firelit figure of Red Heart, carefully grooming the flames, his eyes shining with each dancing imp of light, his face bronzed by the orange and red. I chose the sharpest and the sturdiest pine needle, mostly green with a freshly browning tip. I walked over to Red Heart, half kneeling in front of him, grabbed the stick he was using to stoke the fire, and dropped it fairly and squarely into the fire. I took his right hand and spread out his fingers. One by one, I poked the pine needle into his fingertips till red beads of blood appeared…

"Hey, wake up. The sun has come up." Red Heart shook my shoulders.

The dream I had seemed to be too real to break away from. I must have looked incredulous to Red Heart, staring at him for signs of reality.

"Come on. We need another four or five hours to walk back and catch the bus and then the subway. I want you to get home safely before dark." Red Heart reached out his hand to pull me up. But he did not let go as I stood face to face with him.

"What is it?" I looked into his eyes again. This time he did not avoid it. His gray eyes shone in the sunlight. I could see the amber tint around his irises.

"I want you to make a promise…twenty years from now, we will find each other again. I want to find out what kind of person you become. I hope you would like to know about me, too." There was a depth to his confidence that I had always felt but only realized now. Our hands were still holding each other. So I squeezed his.

"Yes, we will meet again in twenty years on October first."

⚒ ⚒

Nineteen and a half years later…

⚒ ⚒

CHAPTER 12

UNCLE'S COMPANY

The cell phone rang. I tried to open my eyes, but they were dry and hurt for lack of sleep.

I reached over to the nightstand. The blue light pierced my irises.

"Uncle, what's up? It is three in the morning."

"Oh, sorry, I forgot the time difference. But it is very important, and you've got to help me. My company got sued. And the kid attorneys here are struggling. Now everybody wants blood once you are part of a big, global company."

"You got sued already? It has only been eleven months since you merged with GEM Global! This hurts both sides financially and reputation wise." I groaned.

"That's what I am saying. That's why you've got to help me. Besides, the plaintiff is the head of Silkie Farm—Ray. You remember him, don't you? He was one of your elementary-school classmates."

Do I remember him? I thought to myself. *I have not thought about him for more than twenty years.* The thought of him now still brought up the image of those masculine shoulders glistening with sweat and the cold look he cast my way.

"OK, give me a minute to go downstairs…"

"Mom, is it time to get up?" My ten-year-old walked out of his bedroom dragging his blanket along.

"Not yet, sweetie; please go back to bed. It is still night time, and Mommy needs to take care of some work."

⇥ ⇤

"Uncle, tell me more about your local team. Are you sure they cannot handle this?"

"Well, I have two young people here, but they have not seen anything this big. Besides, they are not litigation lawyers. They are compliance, you know. We need big guns. You are the associate general counsel. You have done these things before."

"But, Uncle, my two kids are in school, and I can't travel for a long duration."

"Come during summer months, then. As long as you agree to help, I will get the materials over to you and get you started. The trials are not going to start for a while. Right now, it is depositions and fact-finding. We can telecommute."

The corporate office approved Uncle's request very quickly, and I plunged into the piles of paperwork with much interest and

148

curiosity. It had been almost fifteen years since I had come to the United States to a prestigious college and then law school, passing the bar, joining a law firm, and eventually landing a job at Global Electronic Manufacturing (GEM), Inc. Life had been busy and fulfilling, though not without difficulties and heartache. My husband and my two boys were the ones sustaining me. For them I worked, grew, and loved. The heart softened through daily life and wrinkles came through every smile and grin.

For fifteen years, I had not thought about China, my roots, my ambitions, my dreams, and the promises of youth. I was barely in touch with my immediate family members there. Everyone was busy; everyone was swept up by the changes of the world.

The prospect of returning, even for a short period of time, excited me. It made me anxious, too. Would I be disappointed by what I would find in my homeland? And how would my homeland find me?

Uncle had always been the quirky genius of the family. While his sisters took advantage of the new wave of emphasis on academics and became leaders in education and research, he had a knack for technology innovations. Coupled with his good looks and a charming salesman personality, especially when he was drunk, Uncle quickly stabilized his position at his old textile company. Under his leadership, he transformed it into a multiline production company that used the textile advantage to manufacture batteries for machines, autos, and electronic devices.

When he designed the new portable electric car batteries using maximum load current with layered textile core, Global Electronic Manufacturing was very impressed by the future promises of this compact, plugin, rechargeable, portable car-battery line. They paid a handsome premium to acquire a majority share of Uncle's company while giving Uncle the authority and resources to perfect the technology and expand the campus, readying his product for market. The new marriage of creativity and resources was boding well for both parties. However, the Silkie Farm incident put a huge damper on this newly created joint venture.

⇥ ⇤

It was hard to describe the ordeal of a fourteen-hour flight. The constant food smells mixed with all other kinds of human scents were enough to make me nauseated, not to mention the time-lag effect on a sensitive nervous system suffering from separation anxiety from a world too comfortable and familiar and a home where little ones always tugged at your heartstrings.

Uncle sent a company limo to receive me. It helped ease me into the land where I had grown up and a land with many new surprises waiting.

"You don't recognize me, do you? I am Xiao Liang, your old neighbor." The limo driver looked at me through his rearview mirror.

"Xiao Liang? Yes, of course, it is you. You are working for the company?" I could not hide my surprise.

"I am contracted. I have a taxi medallion. So I could still get other clients. But it has been quite a few years that I've been working for your uncle. It is a good job, safe and stable. Your uncle is a good man, always taking care of people around him. He told me about the lawsuit and the reason you are here. I am sure things will work out. Good people should work things out. Oh, by the way, how is your sister, Nan-Nan? I heard she is in Canada."

"She is doing great." I answered politely, knowing that my sister would be a whole different story.

"Is that your daughter with the violin?" I saw the picture hanging on the passenger-side sunshade.

"Yes, Qing Yin (Clear Light Sound); she's talented, won second prize in the city competition." Xiao Liang's soft voice was filled with pride and joy.

"Wow, congratulations. You guys as parents must be so proud. What does your wife do?"

"Oh, she's a teacher. Actually, she was one of your dad's students. A group of us, all students of your parents, visit your house every year," Xiao Liang said excitedly.

I pondered the words "your house" and wondered when I would be able to visit.

"I will take you to your parents' house this evening." Xiao Liang seemed to know what I was thinking. "But Mr. Zhai asked me to help you settle into your apartment first. The company leased it for you, right next door to the Head Quarter."

The traffic constantly stopped as we got off the city-airport highway. The stop-and-go coupled with my latent jet lag made me feel ill. So I rolled down the window. Even in the widest streets and the busiest districts between high-rises and impressive modern structures, food smells still crept in. There were scents of greasy fried dough, pungent fish stew, fervent lamb chop suey, and sweet sticky rice. For someone who had been living on salads and the occasional Italian for years, my senses were in shock. I rolled up the window again.

It was a big relief when Xiao Liang turned into a narrow inlet and parked the car in front of a tall building at least forty stories high, standing side by side with more than two dozen modern buildings with business signs—IBM, HBC, Intel...

"It is a building for expats mostly. The bottom connects to retail-and-business malls—very convenient. You don't have to come out if you don't want to. You will find out soon." Xiao Liang helped me carry my luggage to my apartment and told me that he would pick me up at 7:00 p.m. to go to my parents' house for dinner.

My apartment was a well-proportioned one-bedroom suite with brightly lit living space, furnished simply but functionally. Realizing it was too early in the morning for America, I e-mailed my hubby and kids about my safe landing.

After the shower, I still had a couple of hours to kill. So I decided to walk to GEM China's headquarters.

"Good afternoon, how can I help you?" The receptionist addressed me in English, which was a pleasant surprise.

"I am Morning Feather Wang, associate general counsel. I am here to see Mr. Zhai," I replied.

"Yes, of course. Please take a seat. I will let him know."

I had barely sat down when Uncle hurried out. We awkwardly hugged. I realized that Chinese people did not hug. But Uncle must have been familiar with the Western customs by now and was unsure as to the proper ways to greet a relative and a colleague.

"Let me take you to your office, then. I did not realize you were coming in today. I thought you'd rest and see your parents first. But good, come with me."

My office was two doors down from his, and Uncle's company seemed to occupy half of the floor. I assumed that real estate must be precious. Although this was apparently a class A building, it was designed with space consciousness in mind, effective and efficient.

I immediately saw the file boxes on the back of the credenza and went to open them. Uncle stopped me. "Morning Feather, no work today, please; rest and tell me about your family. Actually, let me give you a few minutes to settle in. I will get us something to drink." Uncle hurried out again.

I was not sure what to do. So I mindlessly opened up all the drawers and cabinets. They were empty except for basic stationary. I went to open up the file boxes. They were in good order with original lawsuit documents, depositions, lab results, and so on.

"I said no work today." Uncle came back with Tracey, his assistant, each holding a tray. Uncle's tray had an assortment of soft drinks and water; Tracey's had two hot coffees and cookies.

I thanked them. Uncle and I sat and chatted till Tracey came to say good night. Uncle gave me a bottle of wine to bring to my parents later.

I walked back to my apartment, realizing that my entrance key was critical at keeping electricity on. It had to be inserted into the slot by the door to get electricity. I was packing up gifts for my parents in a big bag when Xiao Liang called from downstairs.

⇒⊹ ⊹⇐

Between jet-lagged, sleepless nights and a hard-to-distinguish night-and-day weekend, I managed to get up to speed with the depositions and some historical facts.

Ever since the joint venture, Uncle's branch of GEM was able to secure a manufacturing plant in Huairou, a suburban district northeast of Beijing, just outside of the Sixth Ring Road. The plant used to be a textile machinery manufacture. The main building had stayed vacant for a number of years since the textile business privatized and the market saturated. Uncle's knowledge of the textile industry created the unique opportunity for him to develop it into a new manufacturing plant for batteries, utilizing textile to develop a new generation of batteries that aimed to meet the needs of modern electric cars to microchip mobile devices. GEM Global put the resources behind him and provided loans of twenty million us dollars to retrofit the plant for both R&D and manufacturing.

Huairou was one of the most scenic suburbs in Beijing. Prior to the westernization of the 1990s, it was primarily a tourist attraction. The economy was largely based on agriculture and tourism. As Beijing's population continued to explode, and all kinds of industry set up headquarters inside the Fourth Ring Road, the city's borders expanded. City workers often migrated to the suburbs and traveled to the city for work. As the city's real estate kept skyrocketing in prices, previously deserted factories in the suburbs started to be scooped up by joint ventures and new enterprises. GEM's investment in Huairou had turned out to be very lucrative. It made the product-to-market delivery much quicker. Workers who lived or relocated to Huairou found it a wonderful place to live in without the headaches of traveling to the city.

Huairou had also been the home base for the Silkie Farm for more than thirty years. Silkies are a special species of chicken. They have the most luscious and fluffy feathers that feel like silk. The feathers are mostly tan colored. However, inside the silkies' bodies, the meat is exotically dark, and the bone is almost pure black. This delicacy was on the emperor's menu in the old days. Legend said that it could cure many diseases and, at times, revive the near-dead.

A beautiful piece of land by the Eastern River was home to the thousands of silkies each year. The farm was originally leased by a disabled lady, Mrs. Blue, who married the popcorn man. Silkies provided a livelihood for them. Gradually the small farm had grown into the now "super" Silkie Farm that supplied to many high-end supermarkets and organic grocers. Silkies nowadays were on the menus for head officials from other countries and corporate dinners to household parties. This was a million-dollar industry that would only see growth in the coming years...until the two entities Silkie Enterprise (Silkie Farm's official name) and GEM China clashed in a fatal incident shortly after the Chinese New Year.

On the last night of celebration of the Chinese New Year, an ambulance was called to the Silkie Farm where the plaintiff's family lived. Mrs. Blue was taken to the hospital for acute poisoning of chemical-based solvents, possibly from ingesting contaminated silkie meat. And the farm reported that all silkie chickens were found dead the next morning. Lab results showed high levels of acid-based solvent and nickel deposits, which were the minerals and chemicals used in producing lithium-ion batteries that Uncle's GEM China was making.

Silkie Farm accused GEM China of polluting food and water sources with toxic wastes. Silkie Farm had asked for $5 million in damages and an injunction of GEM China's manufacturing process.

Plowing through the materials got me familiar enough to face the next morning's deposition for Uncle by the opposing attorney. I prepared Uncle for the environmental benefits and relative safety of lithium-ion batteries versus the traditional lead-acid based batteries and the newer nickel-metal hydride batteries.

"Morning Feather," Uncle looked at me, deep in thought, "I cannot afford to lose this case. I borrowed twenty million US dollars, and the company is spending five million each year in salaries and costs developing the new technology, hoping to take a share of the ten- to twenty-billion-dollar market in the next few years. If we lose, we will not be able to open again, now that there are so many environmental restrictions guarding against any new manufacturing in Beijing—or China in general. If we lose, we are marked for death. I do not know what happened to cause the death of the silkies. I have been very careful in waste disposal. It is taken to designated areas for neutralization. We've never even once let any waste leak into public sewage or anything." Uncle sighed. "I was hoping you would be able to talk to the owners of the farm, now that Ray has been the CEO for a number of years. Maybe you can persuade him to settle and avert the bad press and financial costs?"

The mention of Ray's name made me skip a heartbeat. I understood what Uncle was asking me. But Uncle did not know what had happened between us back then. I wondered if my presence would make the situation worse.

"I will try to reach out to him, Uncle," I promised anyway.

━╪ ╪━

I wore my black pantsuit for the deposition. There were decorative bows on each of the sleeves to break away from the corporate stiffness. From the earlier records, I knew the opposing attorney was a man in his fifties, and he was more senior than my previous associates here representing Uncle. I was prepared to talk and engage. I would try to broach a mediation or settlement if I saw the opportunity.

Two people wearing black suits came to Uncle's conference room, a man fitting the description of the opposing attorney and a woman in her forties, short and gaunt, her sharpness cutting through the stale air of the room, making me uncomfortable in every way. I smiled at both, reaching out my hand ambiguously toward both.

The man took my hand and shook. "I am Philip. Allow me to introduce..."

"Julin. I am the head council. I am here to inform you that this is now a class-action suit. I represent seventeen entities in Huairou collectively suing for damages for environmental hazards created by GEM and for an injunction."

"I..." It was hard to contain the shock I felt at the turn of events. This was my first official presence on the case, and now it was a class-action suit representing over $100 million in damages.

"Please take a seat. Would you like anything to drink?" That was all I could say to help me curb my anxiety.

"Water, please," Julin answered curtly. I smiled at Tracey with a nod to let her alert Uncle of the change before he came in for the deposition.

"Attorney Julin, are you here only to serve notice of the change of the case, or do you still intend to depose Mr. Zhai?" I asked softly in a clear voice.

"Both." Julin seemed too proud for words.

"Of course, I will ask Tracey to invite Mr. Zhai in here. In the meantime, please relax. Philip, do you and Julin work for the same firm?" I turned to Philip in the hopes of getting more information.

"Ah, no, actually. My client has decided to consult an expert in environmental law. And Ms. Julin, as you know, is famous for her representation of the farms related to fracking of oil drills," Philip said amiably. Julin shot him a silencing look. Philip looked down, drinking his water.

My heart jumped. The mention of oil reminded me—Julin and the green dance, how could that be? She was a beautifully endowed teenager who could not pull away from food. The woman sitting in front of me was slim, cold, angry, and calculating. Could it be her?

The deposition of Uncle was a pure formality. Julin did not seem to be interested in what Uncle had to say and wrapped up the session quickly.

I knew that the turn of events from a single lawsuit to a class-action suit could mean disastrous consequences for the company. I needed to capture any possibility of reconciliation.

"Julin," I said as she stood up to leave. "Do you remember me? We were roommates at Daqing Oil Field summer camp."

A puzzled look swept over her dark, hollow eyes. A moment of recognition and remembrance was soon replaced with coldness and guardedness. "Yes, it is nice to see you again. Good-bye."

That was not the reaction I expected. My heart sank deeper than I could contain.

The newspaper blasts from all sources made the day even harder to bear. My first official appearance on the case had signi-fied the media-touted class-action suit by seventeen entities. Was I doomed to fail?

CHAPTER 13

A VISIT

I spent the day in the office, studying Julin's profile. It was all over the paper for the last few years. Regardless of the merit of the suit itself, she seemed to be famous for getting the biggest media and governmental attention. She had turned every out-of-context word or random action into an environmental frenzy where her backers kept adding fuel to fire. Whenever she took on ambiguous cases, she had brought the defending companies public condemnation. So the suit was lost even before court hearings.

I was so depressed. Even Uncle avoided coming to my office. He asked Tracey to remind me to go home by closing time.

I wandered out into the darkening street. Amid the impressive glass and concrete buildings, I saw the new moon climbing. Food smells once again permeated the evening air. Laughter and conversations passed me by. I felt all alone. For a moment, I felt so homesick that I could not bear it. I took out my phone, intending to call my parents, but the screen showed Silkie Farm's office phone number. Yes, I was considering calling Ray for an office visit earlier, before I went into that fateful deposition. Now it was almost seven o'clock. Should I leave a message? I dialed the number.

"Silkie Enterprise. Ray speaking." I was startled to hear his voice.

"Ray, this is Morning Feather, your classmate from elementary school. I don't know if you know...my uncle had asked me to come and help him with negotiations." I chose my words carefully.

"Yes, I heard. Negotiations?" He chuckled. "How are you going to do that now that it is a media frenzy?"

"Can we meet and talk, at least to catch up on things?" Now that he understood I was facing an uphill battle with almost no chance for redemption, his sympathy could help me.

"Sure...I am here for another hour or so if you can come by," Ray reluctantly agreed.

"Xiao Liang, I need to get to Silkie Farm fast. Can you come and get me?" My hurried voice must have alarmed Xiao Liang.

"Yes, of course. Wait, it is rush hour now. And it will take me half an hour to get you at your place and another half hour to get out of the city. Can you...I am only asking because this sounds urgent. Can you take the subway to Sixth Ring Road? It will only take you ten minutes once you are on the train. I will wait for you at the subway exit, under the Great Wall Tour sign."

"Yes, of course! Thank you!" I ran down to the subway.

I was very happy to see Xiao Liang waiting for me, his hard driver cap in hand, smiling.

"Thank you!" I was panting from climbing the stairs.

"Oh, thank you! You know I would not have asked you this if I did not know you from before?" he said politely. I patted his arm.

"I am glad you did. Thank you for trusting me." I climbed into the limo.

⚌╪ ╪⚌

"You got here fast! This time of the evening, were you close by?" Ray opened the door for me full of surprise.

"Thanks to a friend. I took the subway to get out of the city first," I replied.

Ray looked at me curiously. "You missed a button," he said slowly and looked away.

I buttoned up my blouse. It must have been all the running and climbing. I could still feel sweat oozing up my forehead.

"May I have a glass of water, please? I have been running."

"I can see." Ray brought out two chilled Evian water bottles from the fridge. I grabbed one right away to drink and realized that I must be gulping as Ray stared at me in amazement.

All of a sudden, I blushed. At this moment, I had betrayed the public image I had spent decades upholding: the elegant, reserved, proud, and confident lady I had always been. But then again, how could anyone here understand what it required to raise two boys in America—the rolling around in laughter, tears, sweat, and physical pain?

I sat down to inspect Ray's office. It was big and beautifully decorated with mahogany-red wood and black-framed modern paintings of feathers, clouds, and branches. Wait, they were all silkie related. That meant that Ray had commissioned these paintings. He must care so much about them. I felt my heart sympathize as I looked back at Ray, who continued to stare at me.

"So why are you here?" he asked.

I sighed, unguarded.

"I had a really tough day today. As you know, the media was all over the place. My first day, but it seems that I am doomed to fail. My uncle is devastated. Even he is avoiding me..."

Ray looked at me rambling on, amused. "But none of this is your fault."

"Tell that to the corporate office. They have to pin it on someone. I show up; things go south. Who do you think they will pin it on?" I felt relaxed now.

"There's a Chinese saying..."

"When there's too much debt, you no longer worry about it; when there are too many fleas, you don't feel the bites," I continued for him.

"Exactly." Ray laughed. "Well, I can appreciate why you would want to come and negotiate with me. Now, it is a class-action suit. It is really out of both our hands now," he said coolly as he sat back.

I nodded and said, "That's why I've decided not to talk about business. You can imagine my surprise when I learned that this is your company. What you have done is impressive. How did you...?"

"Karma, I guess. I was really in a bad place in the early eighties. Got a girl, my wife now, pregnant, and the cement factory shut down and sent us home with four months *lao bao* (social security). I was smoking on the street when Old Xing, you remember him, collapsed from his platform trike."

"The popcorn man!" I gasped.

"Yes, I sent him to the hospital, and he gave me his list for deliveries for that day—fourteen pairs of black chickens. So I called his wife..."

"The Black Chicken Lady," I interjected.

"Yes, I call her Aunt Blue." Ray continued, "So I made Old Xing's deliveries that day and then sent him home after the treatment. He had a stroke and was no longer able to do the delivery work for the Silkie Farm. I was in need of a job to support my new family, so I took it on. Gourmet and health food was on the rise. I started to make regular deliveries to high-end supermarkets. Business was really booming. Old Xing and Aunt Blue pretty much gave the business to me to run. They just took care of the chickens and eggs. Now we are a multimillion-dollar business, hiring a few dozen employees, and our product lines include meat, eggs, and luxury silkie alpaca accessories."

"The building, is this yours?" I started to understand the scale of the business.

"Yes. We got it about twelve years ago when the textile company went belly up. This is their front building, mostly for management and transportation. It is perfect for us. The Silkie Farm is free range next to this building. And your uncle," Ray looked at me carefully, "he leased the old textile-manufacturing plant in the back. Big productions he's running."

"So are you." I smiled at him. Ray seemed to be pleased with the compliment.

"You want a tour?"

"Sure." I stood with him.

By the name of Silkie Farm, you would think "agriculture"; thus the sparkling management and sales offices seemed overly luxurious.

"What do you think?" Ray noticed my silence.

"Posh," I answered truthfully.

"You think I am overdoing it. I know." Ray stopped me from protesting. "I am proud of this. And I want to do more. We just got a couple of export deals. With the Chinese quotas, you know how difficult it is to get into the world market. Now we are finally there. Once the world knows about silkie alpacas, we will be in Milan, New York, Paris...Here, I will show you. He opened an office with a sales display and gallery and picked out a long, fluffy strand of a scarf and put it in my hands. Immediately, cloudlike warmth and softness enveloped my hands. Yet it was so lightweight. I almost questioned whether I had anything in my hands.

"Dad, are you coming?" a voice called from the front door.

"That's my son. He just came back from college. It's good to see you again, Morning Feather; thank you for stopping by." Ray reached out his hand.

I shook his hand and handed back the scarf.

"Oh, it's for you." Ray looked at me closely. Then he suddenly stepped forward and wrapped the scarf around my neck. Neither of us said anything for a moment, for the memories of an evening following our tutoring session flooded back.

We parted for the night.

CHAPTER 14

TRIAL DAY

The media attention was overwhelming and unbearable. There was little sympathy for Uncle's company, an entrepreneurial company that got in bed with an international conglomerate and then built a highly toxic manufacturing plant in a scenic tourist and farming town and turned it into a wasteland. The new class-action suit represented local and national environmental groups' collaborative efforts to curb pollution and antitrust. Who could resist such an appeal?

My motion for a delayed trial date was denied due to the high sensitivity of the issue. I seemed to be hitting walls everywhere I turned, even though, out of the seventeen entities, most of them specialty farms and orchards, none suffered any real damage. The case hinged upon proven hazardous conditions caused by Uncle's company. The evidence of the fatal incident of the silkies and the hospitalization of Mrs. Blue seemed to be irrefutable.

The trial date rolled around before I could fully study all the plaintiffs' profiles. The courtroom was crowded and noisy. There was a moment of silence as I walked in. Suppressed whispers could be heard here and there. I sat down next to Uncle, trying to send an encouraging smile. Suddenly, a roaring cheer and thunderous claps broke out in the back. I turned around and saw Julin. She walked slowly with her head held high and waved left and right to the people in the audience, while the audience cheered her on. She wore a well-tailored sharkskin charcoal suit. The sharp fabric seemed to act like piercing extensions of her bony figure. Unconsciously, I shuddered.

The side door banged loudly, and the clerk announced, "Her Honor Judge Yung-Hong Zhang is presiding."

Judge Zhang sat down, brushed back an escaping strand of hair from her face, and called for the court to begin. For some reason, I felt a familiarity in her gestures. She seemed to be in her late forties. Her sandy-colored hair had just taken on frost in places, and it was carefully tucked into a bun. The few shorter strands that dripped behind her ears softly framed her smooth, round face and created a feminine look. Her official-issue judge's robe seemed to have been tailored on the back and sides to create a neat, clean appearance.

I like her, I thought to myself. *Why does she look so familiar?*

Julin had started to make her opening statement about the case. Her voice was full of conviction and compassion. She stopped at all the right accent points to elicit audience reactions. And the audience, as if prerehearsed, provided on-cue cheers and applause, despite the court clerk's efforts to ensure orderly proceedings.

To counter Julin's accusations of environmental harm, I cited research advocating for Lithium-ion battery's positive impact. By far, it was the greenest battery type ever. To appease to the nationalism flamed up by Julin, I praised the world-class innovative advances Uncle's company had made as a localized joint venture, the hundreds of professional jobs created for the town, the improved economy for neighboring farms and shops due to the inflow of workers and families. The audience seemed to take it in.

Then Julin called Uncle as the first witness.

"Mr. Zhai," Julin asked, "as a world-class company, what measures do you have to ensure workplace safety for your workers?"

I smiled at Uncle. This was one area Uncle's company had done very well with.

"We have formal policies and procedures to ensure work safety. For example, our R&D lab is a class-one-hundred clean lab. Researchers wear protective suits to go into a vestibule for a high-tech wash before entering and exiting the clean room. Our production shop requires protective lab coats, gloves, and eyewear. And we use special vehicles to take our industrial waste to city-designated processing plants to neutralize. I promise—we have never dumped any toxic waste into any public sewage or soil, ever."

"So, Mr. Zhai, your workers have to wear protective suits, gloves, and eyewear. If they don't, what could happen to them?"

"They get disciplined. Violation of safety rules is grounds for termination," Uncle replied.

"That's not my question. Say, Mr. Zhai, if I walked into your production area without wearing any protective gear, what would happen?"

"You could get hurt," Uncle answered without hesitation. The audience roared.

"Leading," I protested. Uncle's face turned purple.

"Your honor, no more questions," Julin claimed victoriously.

Court adjourned for lunch, and I tried to soothe uncle's disastrous response and to prepare for Ray's appearance in the afternoon.

It was over eighty degrees outside, but the courtroom was cold as ice. I carefully took out the silkie scarf Ray had given me and wrapped it around my shoulders as Ray came in with Julin after recess.

It was Ray's turn on the stand, and we looked at each other. He sighed. There was no regret, no confliction, just simple truth. "Silkie Farm is the livelihood for me and our forty employees. For more than fifteen years, this place has been our home and our livelihood. It went from a private farm that supplied a few neighborhoods with the nutritious and medicinal whole silkie chickens to the most important silkie supplier for northeastern China. And it became the first luxury silkie accessory supplier with multiple global contracts.

"On the eve of February nineteenth, our founder, Mrs. Blue, was rushed to the hospital after eating silkies at home. The doctors found lacerations and ulcers in her stomach—esophageal necrosis. The lab results showed traces of acid, cobalt, and nickel, all materials used to make lithium-ion batteries.

"The next morning, all silkies on the farm were found dead. Most of them showed signs of acute necrosis, with skin and stomach lesions. Lab results showed the same chemical traces—materials used to produce lithium-ion batteries.

"This incident was devastating to our farm. We lost all the silkies in one night. As a precaution, we recalled all the eggs sold, stopped shipping products, and canceled all future orders. Our loss was significant, and it affected our current and future viability as a business. We have no choice but to seek damages from the culprit and fight for our survival by asking for an injunction and permanent removal of GEM from our town."

Ray's testimony was genuine, touching. He nodded toward Uncle and me before leaving the stand. I could feel Uncle's heaviness of heart.

Court adjourned to the next day, and I looked over the list of plaintiffs. Tai Chi Institute caught my eye. When I was giving birth to my first son, I was asked to lie on my back but use my legs to lift up my bottom to help with delivery. The nurses were really impressed by how long I was able to support myself in that position. That was the first time I felt the lasting benefit of my early years of Tai Chi practice. Since giving birth, I started to do Tai Chi regularly.

With the case going on and my apparent doom, I probably could use some Tai Chi now. Plus, I had the "license" to discuss with the potential witness. So I walked in.

Fountains and bamboos adored the entryway. I asked to see the headmaster of the place.

"He is not here right now. But the grand master is. Would you like to see him?" the receptionist asked eagerly.

"Yes, that would be great." I felt pleasantly surprised. The young woman went to the back room; I sat down by the koi pond and picked up a magazine to read.

"It is you, Morning Feather. Welcome."

I looked up and could not believe my eyes, "Colonel, it is you!"

I followed the colonel to his Zen garden.

I was even more surprised when I stepped inside. It looked the same as the colonel's old courtyard, except that this Zen garden was indoors, with semitransparent ceilings—the same brick patios, the same bonsai tree, the same three tree trunks that I used to parkour. There was something different, but I could not immediately pinpoint it.

"The sand," he said, as if knowing what I was thinking. "Instead of dirt and plants, I put a sandbox in the middle of the yard. Remember, rather than slapping water, you used sand to train for strength? I adapted it here. Besides, how could this be a Zen garden without a sandbox?" The colonel laughed. Physically he did not seem to have changed at all. He was still his old, strong self. But his laugh told of many changes in life, a life of happiness and fulfillment.

"Colonel, so this is your school?"

"Not exactly. It is my son's. He really runs the place. I am just here, having a grand time…Well, enough about me. Tell me about you. I hear that your uncle's firm is in a lot of trouble."

"And I am the one who's really going to see this thing go bust." I sighed.

"You remember when you were young, you never gave up. You always put up a good fight, and you were always looking at things people ignored. I was proud to be your Tai Chi teacher."

"You were? I thought you hated me. In the whole neighborhood, only you knew how much trouble I was."

"Indeed you were. I have to say you gave me the most headaches. I could not fathom how such a little thing like you could cause so much trouble on the one hand, while having the whole neighborhood thinking you were the little angel on the other hand." He laughed so hard, in a way I had never imagined he could. The laughter had such a calming and comforting effect on me.

"Well, I guess I was both, depending on who you are talking to..." My heart felt warm, for all my misunderstandings, and lingering resentments of the colonel melted away. Now that I was older and wiser, with children of my own, I could start to see Colonel's perspectives.

"Morning Feather," the colonel said as he turned to face me, "keep searching, and keep fighting. If I know you, you will not give up. Just be careful of what you find. It could be something that you may not have been bargaining for."

CHAPTER 15
MISTRIAL

When I got back to the office, Uncle came in to deliver my plane ticket.

"Are you giving up on me?" I asked jokingly.

"No, no that. I promised not to keep you away from your family too long. My two grandnephews, they must miss you." Uncle looked at their picture on my credenza and continued, "So the ticket is for September third, business class. It is fully changeable, refundable. No need to worry. But I got to tell you, though, I learned a lot from the trial today. I have always been lucky. I did what I wanted to do and got help every time I needed it. I look at Ray and couldn't help thinking that I am responsible. I probably destroyed his business, at least hurt it a lot. Maybe it is payback time. So do what you can, but no regrets, whatever happens." Uncle rubbed his eyes and left. I felt for him deeply, and for some reason, I felt responsible for him.

I looked at my ticket and dialed an international call. My husband answered, "I know it's you. Nobody calls this early."

"Well, I got my ticket now, September third. Just a few more weeks, and I will be home. Thank you for taking care of the kids, hon."

"Ah, no problem. It's been wonderful for the three of us. We eat and sleep as we please and make a huge mess and never have to clean up."

"Ha-ha." I couldn't help laughing out loud.

"Sounds like you are doing well, too?"

"Oh no, not really," I said dejectedly, "You might have read some from the papers. Ever since the case turned into a class-action suit, the environmental lawyer turned this into a war against environmental pollution. Her goal is to oust Uncle's company permanently, says that the company causes cell necrosis and other health hazards."

"What are you talking about? Pollution doesn't cause cell necrosis. Whatever is in the air or soil or water is diluted. It can have long-term impact but nothing immediate or acute. You have to ingest a battery directly to have an ulcer or necrosis."

A lightbulb lit in my head, "Huh, you are right! I forgot you are a doctor. I really should have consulted a medical professional."

"OK, great. Now that I helped you solve the case, can I go back to sleep for a couple more hours?" Hubby yawned and hung up. But I could not contain my excitement. I knew that I had found my lucky break.

"Uncle, Uncle, can you stay a bit late?" I dragged Uncle back to his office, though he was ready to call it a day. I told him about my earlier phone conversation. Uncle kept nodding, "I think we are onto something here. I will get someone to research acute versus long-term health impacts. In the meantime, if acute symptoms can only be caused by direct ingestion, then all the chickens must have eaten the chemicals directly. Somebody messed with the chicken feed. It is sabotage. I will get security cameras from our end. Can you get Ray's?"

Considering the timing of Mrs. Blue's hospitalization and the timing of the dead chickens, Uncle and I started to review the security tape from the afternoon of February 19. Bingo! It was the last day of Spring Festival. The plant was closed for the holidays. Only the waste truck came for pickup. Rather than driving away after the pickup, the truck stopped at the back of Ray's Silkie Farm building's loading dock. The camera caught the driver carrying a canister, prying open the loading door, and entering the building.

"We got him!" Uncle and I uttered these words at the same time, just as the telephone rang.

"Hello, Ray, did you find anything?" I grabbed the phone and put him on speaker.

"I am afraid so, and I recognized the guy. Tong Su, do you remember him? Your next-door neighbor. He used to work for your uncle."

"And I fired him," said Uncle. "He cut too many corners. And when employees confronted him, he retaliated. There were too many complaints, so I let him go with severance before the company merged with GEM."

"I will file for charges with the police and document this new evidence in court. This will end everything," I said excitedly.

"Morning Feather, hey…" Ray stuttered.

"What?" I could almost touch success that I was impatient to wait.

"Maybe another day. Have a good night!" Ray hesitated and then hung up.

Uncle was deep in thought. He seemed to want to talk to me. But I had a ton of work to do.

"Uncle, go home. I got paperwork to do." I waved at him and left.

⊷⊶

Excitement kept me working late into the night, and I had the soundest sleep in weeks.

By the time I walked into court, I felt for the first time dignity, confidence, and comfort.

Uncle arrived shortly after, dressed in his most conservative black suit. I eagerly greeted him.

When the plaintiff's team arrived, the court once again erupted in cheers and claps. Ray was dressed in a sharp blue blazer, beautifully tailored to show off his immaculate shape. He waved at the audience as he proceeded to the seat. The gold buttons on his cuffs reflected the morning sunlight into the shadowy corners of the stale courtroom.

Judge Zhang came to her seat almost with a light skip in her steps. Or maybe it was my own happiness that clouded my perception. "Counselors, please approach the bench," she called serenely.

Julin and I walked to the judge's high platform. She looked at us one by one. I detected a little concern in her voice, "Counselors, please remember, this place is a temple for the law. My jurisdiction governs what I can and cannot do, in the matter of the legal realm. What you need to do for your own clients has much more implications. They are citizens in a community. Be careful of what path you choose." The judge smiled at me and I smiled back. Something so familiar, but I could not remember. She waved us away and announced to the court, "Based on the new evidence filed by the defendant, I hereby announce this case a mistrial. Court adjourned." Then the judge stood up, walked to the side door, and disappeared from view, leaving loud noises of cheers and protests behind.

Uncle and I hugged each other. He looked sheepishly happy. "I am very grateful, Morning Feather. What you have done is amazing. I knew I could count on you. Your kids will be proud. Heck, I am proud. I will call your parents to arrange for a party to celebrate…"

I must have been all smiles when I looked around to see Ray. He was finishing up his conversation with Julin, and he looked back at me. It was a look that I didn't fully understand. Then the plaintiff's team, twenty people strong, started to exit the courtroom. It seemed like the whole audience was following them.

I was confused and curious. I took Uncle's arm to follow them a short distance behind. As the grand gate of the courthouse opened, greeting Julin and Ray were dozens of microphones raised in the air. Down below the steps, hundreds of people gathered with signs and posters saying, "Go Away GEM," "Stop Pollution," "Global firms need to take responsibility!" "Give back our beautiful country!" and so on.

My mouth fell open, and I stopped in my tracks. What was happening now? I dragged Uncle to the side, temporarily hiding behind a large column. I could hear Julin's voice echoing.

"We have not given up. We did not lose this battle. The war on pollution has just begun. The citizens of Huairou, our farms, and local business will fight for justice. We will not stop until global bullies are permanently banished from our lands."

"Hello, Ray, you are the prodigal son of Huairou. What do you think about the judge's decision today?" A reporter asked.

A cheer erupted as Ray waved to the audience. Standing on the top platform, Ray's short-cut hair and rugged figure endeared the audience and onlookers. "Thank you for all your support. As you know, we have been a local business for many years. Huairou is our home and our livelihood. We cannot lie down and roll over. I promise to work with all of you to fight for our survival and prosperity. I am delighted to receive the national environmental protection group's support. We will keep fighting until we succeed!" Cheers and claps roared again.

Uncle tugged at my sleeve, "There's a side door. Let's go that way."

Uncle took my arm to lead me to the side door of the courthouse. However, before we could take a step or two, his phone rang. The echoes in the empty court hall alerted the press outside.

"There they are. GEM China's CEO. They are trying to get to the side door…"

"What is it?" Uncle talked on the phone. "A strike? I will be there."

"We need to get to the plant." Uncle said in a hushed voice. We battled our way through a mob of reporters and the fast audience who managed to get to the side door before us. Xiao Liang drove off immediately, leaving the shouting and protesting behind.

"Morning Feather, I just got a call from the plant saying the workers are on strike. And there are a lot of other protesters, professional ones. We have to prepare for the worst. You should stay in the car. But I need to get in there to meet with management, and apparently union representatives. The environmental groups are behind this now."

I sunk in my seat. From the legal perspective, I had won. But that success might have lasted ten minutes. Why were things so complicated? I had worked very hard. I did not even get to celebrate my win at all. And now there was a strike.

The car stopped at the front of the plant, just past Ray's building.

"Xiao Liang, would you take Morning Feather back to the city?" Uncle asked before getting out of the car.

"No, Uncle, I want to go in with you. If the union is there, you need representation," I argued and stepped out behind Uncle.

If there was a mob scene in front of the court house before, the crowds shouting and rooting between the Silkie building and the

GEM China plant was purely scary. Uncle's plant might have hired four hundred employees. But there were at least one thousand people here, many with picket fences and signs. I tried to read the signs to prepare myself. Amid protestors, I could see farmers and hired professional union protesters. They were the ones who had an orderly yet intimidating appearance.

"GEM, go away."

"Pollutants of society must be driven out."

"Worker safety!"

"Better pay, better safety!"

Uncle and I slowly passed through the picket line, walking toward the entrance. The crowd got unruly, and many curse words were uttered.

All of a sudden, an egg hit Uncle in the back. We turned to look. A red tomato hit me right on my shoulder and exploded into seedy blood-red juice. Uncle grew angry and rushed forward. "Who did that? Call the police!" I held him back, trying not to aggravate the protestors anymore.

Red tomato juice crept down my shoulder. I realized that I was still wearing the silkie scarf. It was stained and crinkled. I looked toward Ray's building. Under the morning sun, I could not see anything inside. But I did notice that the shades inside the windows were open. Sadly, I thought, *Is he watching this? Is he behind this attack?*

CHAPTER 16

WHEN IT TURNS TO DARKNESS

Listening to union demands and facing the sanctions of environmental commission for a day could have unnerved the calmest and the most tactful. For me, it was excruciating. The turn of events was so abrupt that I felt God was punishing me, robbing me of hope and my measly little glimpse of happiness. This was my last week here in Beijing. I was supposed to celebrate, have fun, and visit friends and family. Why did God have to do this to me?

When I finally got home, I tried to use a dry-cleaning solution to clean the silkie scarf. Eventually there was only a slight tan stain left. But I could not return the garment to its light fluffy texture. It had now become thin and stiff in some areas. I became obsessed. I brushed and rubbed. It was not working. The once-beautiful silkie scarf was now ruined, stiff, dirty, and lifeless. *Symbolism*

No, I refused to believe it. Today was supposed to be a victory. Today we found the real culprit, the real criminal suspect of the Silkie Farm destruction. And we were taking steps to catch him.

We should all be celebrating. Uncle and Ray, they should be on the same side. The strike could not have had anything to do with Ray. I just needed to communicate with him so we were on the same page again. I dialed Ray's phone number hopefully.

"Hello." Ray's voice sounded gruff.

"It's me, Morning Feather. Hey, can we meet? I want to talk to you about the next steps."

"Err, maybe…OK, I am going to the Executive Club today. How about we meet there? Say in an hour?"

"Sounds good." I was already grabbing my purse and ran to the door. Before exiting, I decided to take the silkie scarf anyway. It was still a little wet from the cleaning agents. I carefully tied it around the handle of my purse.

Traffic was terrible. I decided to take the subway. Crowded, but at least it was still moving fast.

I must have been a whole half hour early. Confident and determined, I knew I would be able to build an alliance with Ray, the beloved local businessman, the prodigal son. That way, the strike and all the misunderstandings would be erased. We would be joined in an enterprise together to build the new Huairou District.

"Hi, I am here to meet with Ray," I said to the receptionist at the exquisitely adorned entranceway of the Executive Club.

"Yes, Miss…May I ask who am I speaking with?" The woman behind the desk exhibited a sweet smile yet a professional distance that could not be overcome.

"I am attorney Morning Feather Wang. Ray and I have an appointment." I also assumed a professional air.

"Yes, of course, Attorney Wang. Ray had arranged for your meeting at Room 201 with refreshments. Just up the escalator to the left."

I thanked her and hopped on the escalator.

It was an elegantly decorated meeting room, probably fit for a small group, five or six. The oblong table had a nice fresh-fruit display. And two place settings were provided.

He remembered I love fruits. This was a pleasant thought. I took the seat by the window and watched the evening sun drown into a tomato-sauce-colored horizon.

An electric-blue Audi in the parking lot looked sparkly in the sunset.

Ray's car! I thought to myself. *He must have arrived early too.* I pulled out my cell phone to dial but there was no signal. I picked up the antique-looking house phone sitting prettily on the credenza and dialed the operator.

"Hello, this is Morning Feather Wang. Would you connect me to one of your member's phone, Ray?"

"Of course, one moment please." The operator seemed to be searching. "Yes, he is in room eight thirty-nine. I will connect you to his room."

As the phone rang on the other side, I became curious. So he had already arrived and is in the *hotel* suite.

"Hello," a woman's voice answered on the other end.

I choked.

"Hello, who is it?"

"Yes, uh, is Ray there please?" I tried to keep my voice plain and calm.

"Yes, he is in the shower. May I ask who's calling?" By now, I had already recognized the dark-toned and somewhat coarse voice. A lump in my throat made it harder to keep my voice even.

"Yes. Would you please let Ray know that his eight o'clock appointment has arrived?"

"Yes, I will let him know."

As I forced myself to say "Thank you," I heard Ray in the background asking, "Who is it?"

"Your eight o'clock. She said. Boy, are you busy—" I heard all of this before the other side went dead. The tone went flat, like that in the hospital, when someone died. And the doctors and nurses all got busy. But the flat tone was so unyielding. It claimed another one in its unrelenting grip.

You have to look at your watch to know how long death persists. It was still five minutes to eight. But then again, time no longer existed in death. Darkness enveloped the last red rim of dusk. All of a sudden, Room 201 became unbearably small, suffocating.

I have to get out of here. I ran out of the room in a panic. Holding onto the handrails of the balcony, I found that a screen of glass with waterfalls partially shielded the view from the lobby and grand entrance below. Descending from the opposite side on the escalator was Julin. A brown crocodile portfolio in one hand, her sharkskin jacket in another, she took a few steps down the escalator to steady herself. Throwing her jacket into the left hand that held the portfolio, she used her right hand to tuck in her shirt into her crisp, smooth skirt.

Tears ran down my cheeks, and fog blurred my view of the waterfall glass. I was grateful for the waterfalls. *May it shield me, hide me, and run over me.*

⊫⊣ ⊢⊨

"Hey, I was looking for you." Ray's hand gently touched my left shoulder. I shuddered and turned to face him in shock.

"Hey, what happened?" Both of his hands were reaching over. I stepped back and wiped the annoying trail of water from my face. Subconsciously, I looked toward the lobby where Julin was now putting her jacket on, ready to step out of the hotel.

Ray followed my eyesight and seemed to be embarrassed for a moment, like a child caught red-handed. Then he retreated to a quiet reserve.

"How about we go to our meeting room?" Ray raised his face to ask.

I shook my head violently and shot him a look of disgust and anguish. It angered him.

"What do you want from me?" he shot back. "You came down here on your high horses to pass your mighty judgment on me!

Have you for one moment thought about me? What I have gone through?" His voice was bitter and enraged. "You look at me as if I am still that prepuberty boy trying to pass the test. So what, you want me to get a one hundred percent on your morality test? But I am never going to be good enough for you, am I?"

I had to turn away from the glaring fire of his eyes. His words echoed in my head and shook my conscience. "Uh, I didn't mean to. Sorry..."

"No, don't bother. I know you judge me. Many people do. But is it so wrong to want to feel something? Not pity or obligation. Is it so wrong to be wanted, for whatever reason?"

I could not bear to look at him. His normally groomed hair was still damp, and it flipped helplessly to one side. His pronounced facial features showed the marks of hard times, even though carefully addressed. His eyes welled up with pain, angst, and uncertainty.

For a moment, neither of us talked.

"Can we sit? I am...I've had a long day." Ray slouched down on the sofa by the wall. I sat next to him. He buried his face in his hands. He seemed exhausted.

"Have you met my wife?" When he talked again, his voice had resumed the calm control. There was softness, as if it unintentionally escaped through a hard shell.

"We got married early. We were only kids. And she got pregnant, so I married her. Almost twenty years now. Regardless of what we were and what we are, she stuck with me through these years. And she raised our son, mostly her. So I don't want to get a divorce. And she's been lenient with me. She doesn't judge me. But..."

He looked at me with a tired smile. "So you came for business, right? What can I do to help?"

I broke into a little laugh and remembered that I did come here for business.

"Oh, finally, I thought you would never lighten up," Ray jabbed, easing the tension.

I sighed again, not sure how to proceed. The questions lingering in my mind went beyond business. "So, this strike thing at GEM China, and the environmental injunction, are you just a bystander? Forgive me, with Julin on the offensive…"

Clouds cast over Ray's eyes again. "I can't say I am not involved. You know, she's determined, and I have no other options."

"What do you mean, you have no other options?" I inquired.

Ray looked at me incredulously. Then he shook his head. "You won, OK! Today in court, you have gotten your victory. But what about me? And the Silkie Enterprise? For twenty years, I worked hard, and I took care of the farm and the people and then—boom—all gone. It may not have been GEM China who was directly responsible. But the toxins came from it anyway. With all chickens and eggs gone, I had to furlough employees. I lost huge market shares this spring and summer. It is hard to build it back up, now that I am cash poor. I wanted to go global with the silkie accessories, but I have no capital, no people, no market access. I am desperate."

Ray buried his face in his hands again. His big triceps bulged at the finely tailored yet purposefully casual plaid shirt. For someone so big and muscular, he looked so small and vulnerable. I wanted to touch his arm, to pull him close and comfort him. But all I could mutter was, "I am so sorry, Ray; I am so sorry."

"About what?" He looked up, managing a grin. "You know this is not your fault. You were just doing your job, a fine job. Your uncle must be very happy. Well, at least about the case. He will have this other headache that I have a little part of, after you leave." Ray pretended a maverick smile; his teeth sparkled in the street neon lights that crept through the wall of glass windows.

"Ray, please. My uncle worked hard, all his life, just like you. This is his only chance, too. I love him. And I..." I wanted to say, *I care about you, too.* But I couldn't.

"Maybe you are right, Morning Feather. I don't know. I just... I don't even understand myself anymore. What am I fighting for and to what end? But I can't seem to stop, either." He inspected me carefully and continued. "In all honesty, I should thank you. I used to resent you for looking down on me. Don't deny it; you still do." Ray gave a wave of his hand. I bit my lips. "But that just might have been the right push for me. I needed to make something out of myself. I wanted to prove to myself that I am worthy. I have tasted success, and it felt good. But it does not change everything, does it?" I could see the mixture of pain and pride, but more poignantly, his helplessness.

I did not know what to say. I twirled the silkie scarf tied on my bag. The silence seemed to be growing with the darkness of night. But neither of us knew how to break it.

"I am sorry the scarf is ruined," Ray said softly. "I will get you a new one. When do you leave?"

CHAPTER 17

THE MIRROR TELLS ALL

W hen I stepped into the GEM China headquarters, applause
erupted. Uncle was holding a bouquet of flowers. After the
evening I had with Ray, I was rather confused by the warm reception from the office.

"Attorney Wang, thank you for the great accomplishment for
defeating this unjust case." Uncle handed me the flowers. "I am
proud of you, kiddo. And I am hosting you and your parents to-
night, to say thank you and farewell."

"Thank you, guys. It was a great team effort. I appreciate the
recognition, but there's still a lot to do." I waved at everyone to go
back to work.

"Oh, talking about a lot of work to do, Morning Feather, can
you give our local counsels your files? They need to prepare for the
environmental injunction meeting this afternoon." Uncle rushed
away.

I went back to the office to sort through the files. Uneasiness
bothered me. Yes, maybe I did what I came here to do. But my job

was not done. GEM China was still in trouble. Julin being the lead counsel, Uncle would have a lot to worry about. Could I just put it aside and leave?

Wu and Zhu came to collect the files. I asked them to wait while I dialed Uncle's number. He was not in the office.

"Uncle, Mr. Zhai, I would like to accompany Mr. Wu and Mr. Zhu to this afternoon's deposition meeting with the environmental lawyers. I am the most familiar with the case, and I believe I can offer some insight."

Wu and Zhu heard my message and high-fived each other. "Thank you, thank you; we really appreciate your help! We have no experience in this. I've been a nervous wreck," Wu mumbled. The quieter Zhu dragged him away apologetically.

Feeling useful and appreciated, I straightened my outfit and prepared for possible questions.

When we arrived, Julin was already sitting at the head of the table with Philip flanking her on the right, close to the entrance. It was awkward for us to walk around the other side so that we could sit by the window side.

I reached out my hand to shake Julin's. She gave an almost nonexistent touch and let go. "It's hard to keep clean, isn't it?" She looked at me with interest, her voice grinding on my nerves.

"What?" I asked dubiously.

"Your white suit. The season is changing. Nobody will be wearing white after this week. Unless, of course, you are going to a Chinese funeral."

I did not expect such obvious harshness of words and felt everyone in the room grow uneasy. Julin seemed rather triumphant. She pressed her elbows wide on the table and opened up her brown crocodile portfolio with a loud bang. Flashes of last night came to my mind, her untucked shirt, the jacket, the portfolio…Ray.

I had to be strong, I told myself.

"I am ready if you are ready, Counselors." I looked at Julin and then Phillip, and I straightened my back. Wu and Zhu subconsciously followed my posture as well.

As far as the investigations went, I could not have encountered a fiercer opponent. GEM China had been cited for seventeen violations, from construction inadequacies to worker safety issues. In America, companies were inspected on a regular basis by regulatory bodies. Typically, the inspectors will work with the company to discuss and help find ways to address the issues. It is rare that a well-established company will face threats of immediate closure for violations or citations. But Julin was different. As the lead counsel for China Environmental Protection Agency, Julin's approach was startling. She was out for blood. She was not going to give an inch to Uncle's company.

It was no surprise that after the hour-long, nonstop drilling, I felt a little drained. My two associates were in worse shape. Even Phillip, who mostly left the offensive questioning to Julin, became a bit restless. On the other hand, Julin's sun-aged but carefully pampered olive skin seemed to glow as the hours passed.

"How about we take a break, Julin? I am sure some of us need to use the washroom, or at least stretch our legs." I managed my collegial suggestion.

Julin looked at me with annoyance and nodded curtly. I could not help an uneasy feeling. An ominous inkling was gnawing at my subconsciousness.

I took my time to organize my notepad and put it in my portfolio. I locked it (my lawyer training) and then went to the bathroom.

I splashed some water on my face to refresh myself. As I tried to wipe my face clean, I saw, in the mirror, Julin coming out of the stall. Her jacket was not yet buttoned up, and she continued to tuck the shirt into her skirt. A flashback came over me like a wave, and it filled my chest with unspeakable weight.

I steadied myself and straightened up in front of the mirror. My memory sought further back, to the time when we were still teenagers and the time before we all had any real burdens of life: Daqing Oil Field—a place where we had met, a place where both of us had found solace and then eventually hope away from the ballet dreams…

"Julin." I turned around to face her. "I know we probably got off the wrong foot before, but how about we start again?" I asked earnestly.

"Start again?" Julin's dark-toned voice seared. "This is not a place to start. This is where we end things." She spoke with a measured determination.

"Julin, please," I pleaded. "We used to be friends. I don't know where I offended you. Please tell me so I can make it up."

"Friends?" She snorted. "We were never friends. You were just some little city brat who was used to getting what she wanted and always pretended the world is a fairy tale. You never understood where I came from. In fact, you never understood any of us, what we have been through. Things have always been easy for you. And these corporate idiots, of course, will send you to swoop in and rescue their pet project. Why are you still here? Aren't you supposed to leave?"

My mouth fell open. I could not believe the rapid fire Julin had shot at me. *Was I so wrong in my perceptions? Was this how the world saw me?* I could not help wondering.

"Julin, I thought we had a lot in common. We loved dance, and now both of us are attorneys…"

"Yet we couldn't be more opposite. Isn't that right?" Julin edged on. "The bottom line is, you don't belong here. OK, fine, you've won your little battle. You can go back to where you come from. You can claim your victory and receive your medal there. And leave us be. You don't matter in the grand scheme of things anyway." She turned away to walk out.

"Wait." I reached out to touch her arm.

She yanked it away. "Stop it. Leave already. Get out of our lives. Stop dangling yourself in front of Ray! Stop preying on his emotions! Don't you have your own family to run to—your little suburban house with white picket fences?" She stormed out, and her heels clunked on the hallway floor like a broken cog.

I stood there, motionless.

I did not know how long it took me to get back to the conference room. But I did know that the whole time, I was afraid; I was terrified. I was afraid to look into the mirror. I was afraid to see whomever I would see in the reflection. I was afraid to go back in, to face Julin again, to sit down next to my associates, to pretend one more time to be GEM China's lead counsel under all those watchful eyes.

Who am I?

⊨⊨ ⊨⊨

"Attorney Wang," Wu said as he poked his head out of the conference room. "Uh, Attorney Julin had another engagement, so she has rescheduled a continuation for next week."

"OK, I am coming." I clutched my hand in front of my chest subconsciously. "Thank you, God." I could not help uttering a prayer.

⊨⊨ ⊨⊨

Xiao Liang drove me toward Huairou at cruising speed. We were opposite the morning commuting traffic. The morning sun peeped through tall buildings and glass windows. The city was like a gleaming beauty waking up. As we passed the Sixth Ring Road, the air started to instill a dewy freshness. Fewer structures were present. If they were there, they tended to sprawl and stretch, rather than shoot upward. The Tai Chi Institute abutted a row of farm sheds where farmers gathered to sell produce, nuts, and mushrooms.

The colonel came to the door to receive me. There was barely anyone inside. We stepped into his Zen garden. The babbling water fountain made the place seem even quieter.

"Jasmine tea or Zhu-Ye-Qing?" The colonel pointed at the round table. He had set out both.

"For today, Zhu-Ye-Qing," I replied.

He smiled. "It was your father's favorite, too."

We sat down, and he poured me a cup. I emptied it. He poured me another one. I downed it again.

"That bad, huh?" This time he did not refill the cup but pushed a dish of edamame in front of me.

I ate and sucked the sea salt on the shell.

"We talked about Tai Chi before. Energy seeks balance." The colonel said thoughtfully.

Like many Chinese people, I did not have the enzyme to process alcohol. My face started to turn red, and my tongue got a little looser, too. "*We* never talked about Tai Chi. You talked at me. I am not sure how much I listened before."

The colonel laughed. "You are right. You were the most stubborn and unyielding student I have ever had. But that's exactly why your father wanted you to take Tai Chi, to learn to yield to force and redirect it. To learn that the softness is more enduring and long-lasting. It will win eventually, if you know how to lead it."

The colonel sipped some Zhu-Ye-Qing, too. "I know you thought you had won yesterday. But it did not change what happened. There is still an imbalance. GEM is out of place in this neighborhood. On the other hand, Silkie Farm grew up in this neighborhood, and it was finally blooming. Don't you see all this pent-up energy going around? Where does the energy want to go? If you can figure that out, you will succeed eventually. "

I grabbed the Zhu-Ye-Qing bottle, filled my cup and drank up. The colonel frowned. "Oh, I see...You feel lost, out of balance for yourself. Ah, that would be harder to get back." He sighed.

"Is it a matter of the heart?" the colonel asked carefully. I did not respond, which told enough.

"The heart is capable of many things. I hope you find its balance, too." The colonel continued slowly, "Do you remember my scar?" He lifted up his sleeve, and a long, pinkish ridge covered most of his forearm. I remembered that it used to be purple. Now that he had gotten older, his skin tone had darkened, which made the scar lighter in shade.

"I remember. I saw it when we did Tai Chi push hands." The memory came to my half-drunken mind. During practice, I was supposed to listen to force, but I was distracted by the scar and lost my stance. In a blink of an eye, I was thrown onto the tea table, which had a potted bonsai tree. The pot broke into pieces, and the colonel was furious. That was when he stated that that was the only thing he had from her.

"The bonsai pot—was that from your wife?"

"Yes, it was. By that time, it had been twenty years since I lived in loneliness, regret, and stubbornness. How I wished that I had swallowed my pride and gone to her." He swallowed sharply, and with much effort, he added, "Forgiven her."

"Forgiven her?" I was intrigued.

"Nobody knows about this. But here's the truth. I was injured in a military mission not long after we were married. A piece of shrapnel cut through my upper legs, and I could no longer have children. My wife, who had been faithfully taking care of me, standing by me for years and years, really wanted children. She asked for adoption, and I refused, saying that if it was not my kid, it would never be my kid.

"For my twenty-plus years of military services, she was often alone, by herself. She endured all this loneliness and maintained our home in Huairou. My last mission was six months long before my retirement. And when I got home, she was showing. She was almost six months pregnant.

"Back then, there was no such thing as artificial insemination, so she would have done it with another man. But she told me that she ensured that nobody knew about this. Not even the father of the child. She begged me to accept the unborn child as our own and raise him together.

"I was furious. I went on a rampage—broke every single wall, every single window in our house—I left her in shambles and never looked back.

"The scar, plus a few more, came from that rage." The colonel gestured with his hands.

I was shocked by his story. And I started to understand his personality all these years.

"I was consumed by anger and betrayal. I lived a solitary life in pain and shame, despite the fact that she kept writing to me, sharing news about the newborn child, whom everybody assumed to be mine anyway.

"Years passed, and she wrote less. I started to feel regret but was too stubborn to reach out. And then in the year that you started to learn Tai Chi, I learned that she was diagnosed with breast cancer, stage four. There would not be much time left for her. I couldn't help thinking that it was my fault that she was dying. If I was with her, I would have found the problem early.

"I spent the last few days with her, and she asked me to take care of our son. I hated myself for my years of stupidity, but I am extremely grateful that we made peace at last."

I watched the colonel, his face seasoned and worn. But there was a peace and spirituality that shrouded him. Yes, indeed, he had changed. But what a story, what devastating situations he had endured.

He smiled at me. "Whatever you are facing, it can't be as bad as mine. You know, when you were my student, I knew you had the makings of a Tai Chi master, or the internal light for a good person. You were just not conscious of it. Besides, you had my kind of stubbornness, too." He laughed and continued, "But make sure that you don't go to the dark places. Once in there, it will be hard to get out."

I thought about what he said and asked, "Can I try your bow and arrow?"

"You know how?" he asked.

"A little. My boys were taking archery. I learned a little as well."

The colonel handed me the bow. I stepped onto the looped side, bent it down, and strung the loose end. I took an arrow from his bag, pulled open the bow, aimed, and released. It was bull's-eye in the middle tree trunk. I handed the bow to Colonel. In a fast motion, he shot one arrow each into the left and right tree trunks respectively, flanking the middle one.

We smiled at each other. I understood.

"Colonel, may I ask what concerns Tai Chi Institute has, if GEM were to stay here?"

Colonel poured me another cup of wine and one for himself, too. "Morning Feather, this is to wish you true success. Your question can be answered by talking to the receptionist, the teachers, and students here."

We toasted each other.

⊨⊰ ⊱⊨

Attorney Wu poked his head into my office. "Counsel Wang? The police called and informed us they have caught the culprit in the silkie-poisoning case, Tong Su. He is being held at the Chaoyang police station, waiting for trial. I thought you'd like to know."

"Yes, thank you, Attorney Wu. Is it possible to visit him?"

"Yes. Wait…you want to visit him?" Wu seemed alarmed.

"Yes…He has my marbles…" I was slipping into the past and did not realize that my answer would not make any sense to the young attorney.

"OK, I will request a visitation permission slip." Wu left, scratching his head.

Xiao Liang drove me to the police station where Tong Su was detained. Peering out the car window at the severe-looking Chaoyang police station, I felt my legs weaken all of a sudden. Sweat from my hands wrinkled the permission slip that I had been holding in my hands. I was not sure why I came. Tong, my childhood neighbor, a child who suffered much abuse, became a bully himself at school and in the streets. But he always kept out of my way. He even helped me once, making a lasso when I needed the mulberry leaves for my silkworms.

"I won't be too far." Xiao Liang detected my nervousness. "I will just be waiting on the other side of the boulevard. Text or call, and I will be here in less than ten seconds."

I stepped out of the car and walked past the hurdle bars in front of the building. The building looked normal. It was hard to imagine that on the backside of this building, with high walls and barbed wire, this place held up to several hundred criminals at a time before their trials.

I swallowed and walked to the gate.

The officer arranging for the visitation was very nice, knowing that I was the attorney on the prosecutor's side. Now I greatly appreciated Attorney Wu's effort in making this an official attorney's visit. Inside the visitation room, there was a big table with chairs on either side. An officer brought in Tong and set him down in the chair.

"So you are the attorney for your uncle," Tong scoffed.

"You have my marbles." Tong was taken aback by my irrelevant answer.

"Yes, I did. I sold them. Probably could have gotten double or triple the money. But I needed money quick"—he narrowed his eyes—"after your uncle fired me."

"Tong, please understand—"

"No big deal. I don't hate you—or your uncle. Actually, Mr. Zhai took care of me for quite a few years. I was just not cut out for the work."

"But why dump the toxic waste?"

"It's Ray. He pissed me off. Never liked him. He was a hooligan growing up. Just because he had some fucking chickens didn't make him the fucking prince. He and his foreign cars and minions…arrogant son of a bitch."

"Tong, please stop. You have a trial coming up. You could use all the sympathy you can get. I am an attorney. I could…"

"No way. I don't want your help. I am going to prison. Probably for fifteen, twenty years."

"You can take a plea bargain and get a reduced sentence, maybe even serve outside—"

"You don't get it. I *don't want* to be outside. At least in prison, I have a bed and three meals a day. And I can 'reform through labor.' Ha-ha, that's what they say. I only need to worry about not getting beat up too badly. Nothing new here." He winked.

Flashes of memories of Tong's father beating him and making him kneel on the washboard made me close my eyes.

"You are thinking about him, aren't you? My dad?" Tong looked at me intently.

"Yeah." My voice sounded like a whisper.

"Good, 'cause I put him in a nursing home. I broke his legs. Now he has to piss and shit in his pants." Words came out of him like bullets, and I was shocked motionless.

"Time's up." The police officer standing by the window tapped on the door, his electric baton swaying on his belt.

Tong got up, grinning at me. "Thanks for the visit. You didn't have to. But thanks. Oh, if you ever see my dad, he's at the Yanqing Nursing Home; tell him I will see him in hell." He walked out, laughing.

I was chilled to the bone.

⇒⊰ ⊱⇐

"Xiao Liang, would you take me to the Yanqing Nursing Home?" I said in the car, trembling.

"Are you sure, Morning Feather? You don't have to do this, you know. We grew up together, all of us. Some things we cannot control. Some people cannot change. There is no need to torture yourself like this. You should let it go."

But I couldn't.

Xiao Liang sighed as he opened the car door for me by the entrance of the nursing home. "I will wait right here," he said.

The smell of urine mixed with cleaning supplies slapped me right in the face as the double door opened automatically. However, the place looked clean and tidy, better than I expected. I was directed to an old man in a wheelchair in the corner of the living room, watching TV. He heard me approaching and turned around.

"Hey, beautiful, are you an angel taking me to heaven?" The slothful, wrinkled man in a plaid robe opened his mouth, showing his half-remaining yellow and black teeth.

"No, I am your old neighbor, Morning Feather. And you look like hell." I watched his hands twisting his immovable legs.

"I am not far away from hell, either. He-he. Maybe I get to take you with me."

His torso and lower body formed an unnatural angle as he laughed. The images of Gray-Gray struggling in his hands, the flame-colored rooster oozing blood into my washbasin, and the pig-blood letters dripping upon Xiao Liang's back wall, one by one, flashed in front of my eyes. I wanted to shout at him at the top of my lungs, *You are a cruel and evil man! You've hurt so many people around you. What's worse is that you have ruined your own son's life! You should rot in hell!*

I seemed to hear Tong's words echoing: "Tell him I will see him in hell!"

But as I watched him, his evil laughter had set him hacking and choking in his chair. The oxygen tube that was attached to his nose had come loose, and it swayed in and out of his nostrils as his body shook with his coughs. I was filled with pity and disgust. *No, he is not worth it. Just like Xiao Liang said.* There was no point in wasting even an ounce of emotion on him. There was no point in giving him the satisfaction of letting him know people had suffered because of him.

I bit my lips and calmly said to him, "Hope you live a very long life." And then I turned around and walked out of the nursing home.

CHAPTER 18

THE RIGHT THING TO DO, AND I DO IT FOR YOU

⇒⟨ ⟩⇐

"Sweeties, Mommy's got to ask for your understanding to delay my return by four weeks. There's something I must do before going back home...You promise you'll be good and get ready for a new school year? Take care of Daddy Bear, OK?"

⇒⟨ ⟩⇐

Xiao Liang took me on my daily trip to visit a farm in Huairou. The mushroom farmers, Lin and her husband, Bai, received us. Their farm sat further away than most, almost into the mountain and gorge area. The air smelled dewy, and a shadowy chill, uncharacteristic of summer or early fall, covered the long stretch of mushroom fields.

"The mushrooms need moisture and coolness to grow better," Lin explained, showing me a large ear of nature's rare stem. It looked like a donkey's ear; it even had white hairs.

"Although mushrooms are hardy things, the quality of the soil will really affect their growth. As you know, we were concerned about any toxic waste getting into the soil. But with your new proposed monitoring equipment and free analytical services, I think we will be able to grow more and grow better. Maybe eventually we can break into the national market, too," Lin said excitedly.

"I hope so. Please know that GEM is committed to environmental services as well as promoting local farming and other community initiatives. We are just a phone call away. Or you can drive over to the battery plant's new community-and-environmental-service department. They will provide a portfolio of free services to our Huairou communities."

⇥⊹ ⊹⇤

It had been weeks since I started my mission. Finally, I felt ready.

Punching in his phone number, I could almost hear my heart beating.

"Hi, Ray."

"Hi...Oh—Hi, where are you calling from?" Ray asked.

"Here, in my office. Oh, you mean...I am still here, in Beijing."

"Oh, I didn't know. I thought you left...without saying good-bye..." There was delight in his voice. For me, it was a relief to learn that I would have been missed if I had left without saying good-bye.

"Ray, I have been working very hard since we last saw each other." I could not help remembering the circumstances, and holding back a sigh, I continued, "I think you might like what I have prepared for you here. Do you want to meet and discuss?"

"Sure, I have a meeting in the afternoon in the city. I am trying to pitch the silkie accessories to Jing Mao Tower. I have time afterward. Where do you want to meet?"

"How about my office then? You've never been here yet," I said quietly.

"Yeah, OK, I understand. And I will see you there."

I thought I heard him chuckle. "Till then." I hung up the phone and went to Uncle's office to make arrangements with him.

⇌ ⇋

When Ray arrived, I had coffee and bottled water prepared in my office.

"Hey, I was going to give you this, but I thought you had left. So, here." Ray brought out a space-dyed silkie scarf with pale tans, pinks, and blues.

I put it around my neck and wrapped it once. It was so soft and pretty. I pulled it more open and wrapped it on my head.

"Oh, I am sorry. It is so beautiful; I could not help wearing it different ways," I apologized to Ray, who had been sitting there quietly sipping his coffee, watching me.

"No, not at all. The pleasure is all mine!" He smiled slyly at me.

"So how did your meeting go this afternoon with the buyers at Jing Mao?" I asked.

"They are interested and took some samples. They will let me know next week. So, you said you want to discuss something?"

There was a knock on the door, and Uncle came in at my gesture.

"Hello, Ray, welcome! I just heard that you are visiting today, and I wanted to stop by to say hi. Please don't hesitate to ask for anything, OK? I mean anything. I know my Morning Feather will take good care of you. But if you need a factory guy like me to carry some weight or something, don't be a stranger. My office is two doors down."

Ray apparently was very happy with the warmness Uncle had shown. After Uncle left, I asked Ray to come around my desk so that we could see the computer together.

"Are you ready?" I asked him with unmasked excitement…and a little nervousness.

"Yeah, OK. What have you got?"

I unveiled the best PowerPoint presentation I had ever made in my life: "Silkie Farm's Second Coming—from local distribution to global markets, from groceries to fashion frontier." All this was packaged comprehensively under the leadership and control of Ray, with financial assistance and marketing power of GEM China and GEM Global.

I meticulously went through the slides, the executive summaries, and then the accompanying financial document and legal drafts. Ray looked on in awe. By the end of the hour, he sat back, stretched out, hands behind his head, his thoughts faraway.

"Am I being too presumptuous, Ray? Is this OK?" I asked tentatively.

"Yes, yes, it's more than OK. I just don't understand why." He inspected me carefully.

"Oh, one more thing. As a partner to GEM China, you will also have a seat on GEM China's governing board. If you agree, of course…" My voice trailed off, intimidated by the faraway yet intense look on Ray's face.

"Why are you doing this?" Ray's voice resumed the cool, calm control.

"Doing what?"

"This rescue plan of Silkie Farm, low-interest loans and channel access, resources. What's in it for you?" Ray pushed on.

"It is my job," I answered automatically.

"No, it's not. You job ended when you dismantled the lawsuit. And I hear that the environmental injunctions are being handled by local lawyers. This, this plan, is more than a job. Don't get me wrong, I am impressed. I am flabbergasted. It is too good to be true. But why?"

I sat back in my chair. I had worked day and night for weeks now. I never really truly asked myself why. "Because it is the right thing to do?" I was not sure whether I was answering the question or asking one.

"Am I the only one being offered a deal like this?" Ray asked.

"No. I worked on seventeen different offers for all the plaintiffs in the suit. But yours, of course, is the most complex. Corporate had to do a risk analysis before I could present this to you." For once, I felt like a student in front of Ray.

"I am going to need a drink," he said.

⇌ ⇌

The bar downstairs was chic and quiet.

"I am buying. What would you like?" Ray asked.

"Nothing. I don't drink."

"Of course you do. Don't you remember that you downed your mother's whole jar of Jiu-Niang in one sitting, and you were out for a day and half?"

"What? How did you know?"

"You told me. You were a chatty little tutor. You also told me that Qing-Diao beer has the best malt flavor in the world. That comment cannot possibly come from someone who doesn't drink."

"I..." I blushed. "I cannot believe you remember all that."

"Believe me, some days I wish I did not, either. But, hey, here we are. Bartender, a bourbon for me, and Zhu-Ye-Qing for this young lady."

Ray turned around to face me, "Yeah, I remember Zhu-Ye-Qing too. You said you liked the clean taste. And you identify with it— the bamboo, it bends but never breaks." He reached out, opened my palm, and put the shot of Zhu-Ye-Qing in my hand.

━╬ ╬━

The partnership agreement between GEM China and Silkie Enterprise was scheduled to be signed on Friday, September 30, in the morning. An official joint press release would follow immediately after, strategically planned at Ray's office. Later in the evening, GEM China would host all Huairou community leaders for a banquet at the manufacturing plant, featuring local fresh foods.

I prayed that everything would go smoothly. Next Monday, I would be getting on an airplane heading back to America. School had started for both kids. It felt strange that I had not been the one sending them to school every morning.

For almost a month, I went back and forth with every partner-entity in Huairou regarding their MOUs (Memorandum of Understanding) and partnership agreements. People were no longer parties in a now-nonexistent lawsuit; they were now collaborators, advocates, and community members. For my dozen years in my career, there had been nothing so close to the fulfillment I was feeling lately.

It was a gorgeous Friday morning. The crisp air lifted the beautiful space-dyed silkie scarf on my neck. The ends of it flew up into the north-turning wind as if trying to catch its whisper. Sometimes it tickled my chin, replaying back a secret wish.

I could not help the butterflies as Uncle and I walked into the Silkie building. Ray met us just as we stepped outside of the elevator.

"That's a new one." Ray pointed to my hair.

"Oh yes, one of the silkie feathers fell off the scarf, so I glued it to my hair clip. See, my plain old hair clip became a fashion statement!" I proudly tilted my head for all to see. Uncle eyed me with interest.

"Remind me to turn this into a product line—simple and stylish. It will be a hot item for sure. Wait, you are not going to charge me for a patent fee, are you?"

"Didn't have time to file a patent, but give me a bottle of Zhu-Ye-Qing, and we will call it even."

Ray shook his head naughtily and led us into his conference room. The three of us sat down close to each other, and I laid out three copies of the partnership agreement, which both sides had the opportunity to review, negotiate, and revise.

"I am very happy for this day, Ray. I know I have been slaving in this business for thirty years. Now with you, I have a partner who is young, capable, and visionary. You don't know how happy I am!" Uncle exclaimed.

Ray was touched by Uncle's outpouring of sentiments. "What you said means a lot to me, Mr. Zhai. You know, after the disaster earlier this year, I thought I was done. I never imagined I would be able to come back here and do this again—more importantly, with you together. Your experience and resources opened up all the possibilities. And of course…" Ray turned around to look at me.

"We could not have done this without Morning Feather." Uncle and Ray said it together.

I took the compliment with a lighthearted smile and took out the ink pens for their signatures.

"Stop, Ray!" The door swung open. Julin jumped in front of Ray and shoved the agreement back down onto the table.

Ray looked at her incredulously and took back the agreement. "What are you doing, Julin?"

"Trying to stop you from making the biggest mistake of your life!" Julin ripped away the agreement from Ray's grasp. "Don't you see? This is all part of their corporate ploy to get you to play ball with me. You are signing away your freedom. You are signing away the company that you have worked for your whole life!"

"But I am not. I don't have much of anything left if I don't sign this agreement. What do I have to lose?" Ray watched Julin in aggravation.

"It is all a bunch of bull, Ray. All these low-interest rate loans… They can say yeah or nay to everything you do, yet you are still on the line to deliver. They are not doing you any favors." Julin urged on and pressed her hand on Ray's right shoulder.

I inconspicuously fetched back the copy of the agreement that Julin had pushed away from Ray and said softly, with warmth in my tone, "Ray, this is your big opportunity—the one you've always dreamed of—to take Silkie Farm to the global market. You have worked too hard to see it all go away. GEM is giving you a hand to help you start up again, without interfering with your management decisions. Consider us a helping hand, a resource for you. We are here for you." I slid the agreement in front of Ray and gently touched Ray's left arm.

Ray looked at my hand that was touching his arm and then looked at the one from Julin, heavily on his right shoulder. Everyone in the room seemed to notice this—everything seemed to be hanging in balance. I was not going to give up. My hand was warm and gentle, and my smile was trusting and encouraging.

Ray reached out his right hand to receive the ink pen from me. Julin abruptly pushed his elbow onto the conference table. "Ray, as your attorney, I advise you *not* to sign this agreement."

"But you have never been my attorney, have you?" Ray looked at her coolly.

"You son of a bitch!" Julin's hands landed a violent push on Ray's shoulder, and she turned and stormed out of the conference room.

Even in the surprising commotion, I did not give up my support for Ray. His upper body violently jerked toward me. I held him steady with my body. And then in a swift, gentle motion, I helped him recover his balance.

Ray put his signature on the dotted line; Uncle did too. They exchanged their copies, repeated, and then they stood to shake hands.

I watched in silence, with a quiet smile on my face. Nothing could make me happier. I felt life had meaning. I felt I was part of something big...

The press conference that followed was a beautiful affair. It was strategically designed to showcase Ray's office, a local entrepreneur and a prodigal son from humble backgrounds. His desk was covered with a specially designed cloth that combined the two companies' logos in a tasteful manner together.

Under the limelight, with only a few key executives attending from both sides, Uncle and Ray each read their statements of intent and shook hands, holding the signed agreements for cameras and videos to feast on the occasion.

Following this part of the well-executed plan, the parties walked together to GEM China's manufacturing plant and entered the flower-and-ribbon-decorated conference center turned banquet floor. The blue and silver ribbons meshed well with Ray's dark-blue blazer. And the abundance of fruit and flower displays balanced out Uncle's meticulously groomed black boardroom suit. More than three hundred people attended the banquet. Local governmental officials, business owners, and key employees who were part of the stakeholders, gathered together, chatted, and enjoyed fine foods and local delicacies.

I never cared for the limelight. Now that everything seemed to be in motion, and everyone was enjoying the biggest moments in Huairou's history, I felt the need to retreat to my own world. Yet, in a sea of people, I was carried by the wave, unable to break free.

*Ding-dong...*Saved by the bell.

"Hello, this is Morning Feather," I answered.

"Morning Feather, I am Yung-Hong. I've been wondering whether you still remember me."

"Judge Yung-Hong?" I held my breath. "You mean you are Liu Yung-Hong, but Zhang Yung-Hong now, my childhood friend?" Hearing these words coming from my mouth opened a floodgate. But I could not choke in front of so many people.

"Where are you?" I asked. "Of course, I can come and meet you. I will be there in forty-five minutes." I hung up the phone and looked for Uncle.

"Uncle, I have something to take care of. You don't need me for anything else, right?"

"Oh, I am good. Something I can help with, Morning Feather? You should be celebrating here. You know how important you are in all this."

"Another time, Uncle. Thank you." I waved good-bye and pushed my way through the crowds toward the entrance. I stole a look back at Ray. He was raising his glass with a few local farmers, his cheeks flushed and demeanor, happy.

I put on my coat and began buttoning it up and almost ran into Ray head on.

"I saw you coming out. Are you not staying?" he asked with a glass still in hand.

"Something came up that I need to take care of. I am sorry." I wanted to rush away, not to be impolite, but Yung-Hong was waiting.

"Hey." Ray grabbed my arm. "Wow, it seems that you are running away from me. Look, I never thanked you. I mean, you have given me my life back and more. I need to properly thank you."

"Another time, Ray, please? I am kind of in a hurry," I begged.

"OK, OK. But promise me, all right, that you are not going to leave without saying good-bye. You *will* let me thank you properly! Promise me!" Ray insisted.

"Yes." I took his hand off my arm. "I promise."

⊫⊰ ⊱⊪

I met Yung-Hong at a teahouse not far from the courthouse.

"You changed your last name?" I asked.

"Yeah, my mom and dad eventually split. They were not the most cordial with each other. So I went with my mom's last name, because I never really knew my father to begin with."

"I don't remember ever seeing him either," I said, smiling. "Judge Zhang! How grand."

"Says the big corporate lawyer," Yung-Hong shot back.

The server brought us a couple of desserts.

"Oh my God, this is the sesame thousand-layer cake!" I exclaimed.

"Yep, all thanks to me, now it has your name on it." Yung-Hong pointed to the menu behind the counter. There it was: "Morning Feather Cake."

We shared with each other pictures of our kids.

"Your boys are so cute. Here is mine, almost a young man now." Yung-Hong took out a picture of her son, and another picture fell on the ground. I went to pick it up.

"Hey, you have a cat. What's his name?" I exclaimed, admiring the fuzz ball.

"*Her* name is Gray-Gray." Yung-Hong looked at me thoughtfully.

I felt a lump in my throat. I looked at Yung-Hong and her escaping sandy hair. Tears welled up. She came over to me and put her arms around me.

⚞ ⚟

"Oh, I am organizing a party at my house tomorrow, to celebrate National Day, October first. Would you come?" Yung-Hong asked as she got into her taxi.

"Yes, of course! I will be there!" I waved good-bye to her.

Suddenly I remembered. October 1, twenty years ago, I had made a promise.

Where are you, Red Heart?

CHAPTER 19

FAREWELL

"Morning Feather, are you all packed yet? Do you need any help?" Uncle asked anxiously.

"Uncle, I am not a kid anymore. Everything is all set. I don't know why you are so worried." I patted his arm reassuringly and got ready to exit the limo.

"Oh, I feel guilty to have kept you from your family longer than expected. Besides, I promised your mom and dad at dinner to make sure you get on that plane tomorrow safe and sound."

I got out of the car and turned around. "Thank you, Uncle. You *have* taken good care of me here. I will see you tomorrow morning, OK?"

The limo drove away as Uncle waved good-bye.

I took out my key card and walked toward Fortune Tower, my home for the last three months. For most of this time, I felt the days and nights were as slow as slugs. Now, the night before I was about to leave, it hit me how fast and tumultuous yet quiet and peaceful things had been.

I looked around at the strange shapes of the buildings in one of the busiest districts in Beijing. They seemed to be sleeping in the darkness, most of their lights and sounds turned off. Few people walked about in the dim and sparing remains of street lamps. The darkness drew your eyes to the sky. It was a sparkly one, very rare in the now heavily polluted city. Stars twinkled here and there in the ink sky.

All of a sudden, I could not help my tears.

I put the key card back into my pocket and waved to a cab.

Standing in front of the Silkie building, my resolve was wavering. Darkness was all I could see. The whole building, standing in the cross fires of streetlights and the moon, was dark, solemn, and silent. The depressing atmosphere pushed against my chest, and I couldn't breathe.
I raised my hand hesitantly. I rang the buzzer.

"Hello?"

Startled by the voice from the telecom unit, I had to look up again at the building. It was still in darkness.

"Hi, it is me, Morning Feather." My heart quickened as I spoke. The buzzer sounded with a clunk of the door latch opening. I took the elevator to the second floor, and the door slid open to Ray's overpowering stink of alcohol.

"Oh, gosh..." His shadow startled me again.

"Hello." He breathed heavily into my face. I turned my head away. "I didn't know you were coming. Sorry, I am not dressed for the occasion. You said you couldn't make dinner or what-ever…" Ray's speech was severely slurred, and a pang of regret hit me.

"Are you OK?" I rushed to support his arm.

"Oh, a little tipsy, am I?" He laughed and stumbled with me to his office.

I automatically turned on the light.

"Ah!" In the moment of brightness, Ray's arms flailed in the air to cover his eyes.

I had to turn the light off again. An almost-empty bottle of whiskey on his desk caught my eye before things went dark again. It took a moment for my eyes to adjust to the surroundings. The streetlights outside shone just enough light into the floor-to-ceiling windows.

"How much did you drink?" I tried to steady him again.

"Not nearly enough, ha-ha. You want to join me?" He stumbled forward.

"No. Ray, stop; you are drunk."

"Am I? If you say so." He pushed himself straight against the small round meeting table. "What are you doing here, anyway?"

"I…I came to say good-bye."

"Hooray, that's an occasion worth celebrating." Ray once again stumbled toward his desk. He grabbed the whiskey bottle in one hand and lifted it to pour into his mouth.

"Stop, Ray, stop!" I ran into him and wrestled the bottle out of his hand. "You can't drink any more. You are hurting yourself!"

"Whiskey doesn't hurt me. You do." Ray reached for the bottle in my hand, and we got into a real tug-of-war.

"Ray..."

"You"—he firmed up his grasp on the top of my hand and would not let go, staring at me like a maniac—"don't know how much you hurt me." His hand was burning hot on top of mine, and the bottle felt ice-cold under my palm. "No amount of liquor can drown out this pain!" he shouted.

I burst into tears.

The bottle fell. I guess I lost my grip when I lost my composure. The clunk was muted as it hit the plush carpet, but the splash of liquid hit my legs. Offensive malt and alcohol smells filled up each of my choking breaths.

I felt that I was going to fall like the bottle.

"Hey, I am sorry. Are you OK?" Ray put his hand behind my back and pulled me close.

"*No!*" I could not stop crying, and I couldn't talk. My chest heaved uncontrollably, and every time, it cut off my breathing. I thought I was going to pass out.

"Sh...sh...it's OK. It's going to be all right." Ray gently rubbed my back and laid my head slowly against his chest. For once, the mixture of sweat and alcohol did not repel me. My breathing started to return.

Gradually I felt I had enough strength to stand on my own again, so I tried to push myself away.

"Woah, dizzy," Ray mumbled. "Give me a second," he added.

Gently led by him, the two of us moved slowly toward the door, and then we both slid down to sit on the floor, backs against the door. For a while, neither said anything. There was the thumping of the engine outside retreating farther away, and the silhouette of the trees swayed on the window. But the wind was too quiet and timid. Even if it was there, we could not hear it.

"Give me a minute, OK?" Ray lifted himself up and walked to the mini fridge. He took out a bottle of Evian, splashed himself on the head, and then drank the rest. Turning to look at me, he fetched me another bottle.

Ray sat himself down, shoulder against the door, half facing me. He took my hands in his, holding them tight, deep in thought. Finally, he looked up at my face. There must have been remnants of tears there. He reached over and wiped them away.

"Thank you for coming," he started out with a bittersweet smile. The tenderness in his voice caused another stream of tears.

"Oh, hey, no more crying...I am sorry. I've been selfish." He shook his head. "For the last three months, you've given me so much. You have given me my life back. No, you have given me a new life. I should be very grateful...I am. I am sorry I wanted more." Ray sighed.

"You don't know how much I love you and how long I have loved you. I wanted the moment of truth with you. I dreamed of having you." Words came out of him like a babbling brook. I listened without protest. Ever since I walked into his office, the gate of my heart was breaking down. I finally let the fear go and let the exhaustion overtake me. Now, sitting in the darkness facing him, I was a blank slate, open and defenseless.

"But I can't have you, can I?" He touched my face again and brushed back an escaping strand of hair. "That would ruin your life, wouldn't it?" he asked in a whisper, a mixture of hope and despair seeping through every word.

There were no answers in the wind. If there was wind, it kept quiet, motionless.

Ray sat back against the door again. He put his arm around my shoulders and pulled me next to him.

"Tomorrow, you are getting on that plane. And very soon, this will fade into memory." He turned his face to look at me while stroking my hair. "A memory that I will treasure till the end of time." Ray's voice trailed into a whisper.

"Look, it is a comet!" Ray exclaimed. "Make a wish!" The flash of the cool celestial light flew past the window and disappeared into the edges of earth and sky.

"The comet makes me think of you." Ray looked at me once more. "You appear for a short period of time and give people hope, and then you disappear again. For the lucky ones who had the chance to wish upon you, you make their dreams come true."

The End